"As soon as we shove the dummy out, start screaming," Frankie whispered.

We looked out. Mom and Dad were sitting on the deck one floor below.

"Maybe this isn't a good idea," I said. "What if they think I really fell?"

"Quit worrying," Frankie said. "Mom and Dad are going to think this is hysterical."

Hysterical. Ha! Mom and Dad were hysterical all right . . .

Here is what happened: Frankie and I shoved the dummy out my window. As soon as it cleared the windowsill, I started screaming at the top of my lungs. . . .

Frankie leaned out the window, pointed at the dummy, and shrieked, "Julie! Julie!"

Mom and Dad dropped the newspapers as they leaped from their chairs. . . .

By the time I got downstairs, Mom had given our address to the 911 operator and was rushing toward the dummy on the grass. . . .

"Is she alive?" Mom shouted to Dad. The fear in her voice made me feel guilty. "Can she talk?"

Dad stood looking down at the dummy. "Our daughter is not injured," he said. "Yet. . . ."

Books by Peg Kehret

Cages
Danger at the Fair
Deadly Stranger
Horror at the Haunted House
Night of Fear
Nightmare Mountain
Sisters, Long Ago
The Richest Kids in Town
Terror at the Zoo
FRIGHTMARES™: Cat Burglar on the Prowl
FRIGHTMARES™: Bone Breath and the Vandals
FRIGHTMARES™: Don't Go Near Mrs. Tallie
FRIGHTMARES™: Desert Danger
FRIGHTMARES™: The Ghost Followed Us Home
FRIGHTMARES™: Race to Disaster
FRIGHTMARES™: Screaming Eagles
FRIGHTMARES™: Backstage Fright
The Blizzard Disaster
The Flood Disaster
The Volcano Disaster
The Secret Journey
My Brother Made Me Do It
The Hideout
Saving Lilly

MY BROTHER MADE ME DO IT

PEG KEHRET

Aladdin Paperbacks
New York London Toronto Sydney Singapore

This book is a work of fiction. Any references to historical events, real people, or real locales are used fictitiously. Other names, characters, places, and incidents are the product of the author's imagination and any resemblance to actual events or locales or persons, living or dead, is entirely coincidental.

First Aladdin Paperbacks edition June 2002

Text copyright © 2000 by Peg Kehret

ALADDIN PAPERBACKS
An imprint of Simon & Schuster
Children's Publishing Division
1230 Avenue of the Americas
New York, NY 10020

Printed in the United States of America
10 9 8 7 6

ISBN 0-671-03419-7

For my brother, Art Schulze,
with love and admiration

Acknowledgments

My thanks to Ann Kunkel, Education Coordinator at the University of Kansas Medical Center Pediatric Rheumatology Program, who reviewed my manuscript and suggested ways to make my references to juvenile rheumatoid arthritis more authentic. Thanks, also, to Beth Axtell of the Arthritis Foundation's national office in Atlanta, and to Barbara Wade of the Washington/Alaska Chapter of the Arthritis Foundation for invaluable assistance.

MY BROTHER MADE
ME DO IT

September 12

Dear Mrs. Kaplan,

Hi. My name is Julie Welsh. My teacher, Mrs. Lumbard, assigned me to be your pen pal.

Here is what I know about you:

1. You are eighty-nine years old.
2. You live in Kansas at the Shady Villa Care Center.
3. You never get any mail, which is why you are in our fifth-grade pen pal project.

You will probably be sorry that I got assigned to you because I am not a very good letter writer. Mostly I like to read, do crafts, and play with my cat, Itty Bitty Kitty. I used to roller-skate a lot, but lately my legs have been achy, so I don't skate much anymore. Mom says I have growing pains.

Oh, yes, I also hide from my little brother, Frankie.

Now, don't jump to conclusions and tell me I should not hide from people. You don't know Frankie. He is the sneakiest, most devious boy in the world, and if I do not stay away from him I end up in a heap of trouble and get blamed for tons of things that are not my fault. Any time I am in hot water with my parents, you can bet it's because Frankie made me do something wrong.

My dad is an engineer. My mom works part-time as a dental technician. Yuck. I would not want to scrape tartar off people's teeth, but Mom says she likes to meet new people and help them stay healthy.

We are supposed to ask questions in these letters, so here goes. What is your favorite food? Where did you live when you were my age (eleven)? Do you have any kids?

Mrs. Lumbard said you never get mail. Does that include junk mail? If so my mother would like to know how you manage that. Every day she gets a bunch of letters that go straight in the recycle bin, and every day she complains that they are a waste of time and trees.

Please write back. I never get any mail, either.

Your new pen pal,

Julie

September 16

Dear Mrs. Kaplan,

Thanks for writing back so soon. It was fun to get your letter. Maybe this pen pal project won't be boring, after all.

It's too bad they never serve enchiladas at Shady Villa. I would get tired of mashed potatoes and vanilla pudding, too. I'm sorry you have arthritis in your hands and can't write much, but a short letter is better than none, which is what I usually get.

When I asked where you lived when you were my age, I expected you to say someplace near where you live now. I had never heard of the Isthmus of Panama. I looked it up on the map, and it seems very narrow. If you stood in the middle, could you see the Atlantic Ocean in one direction and the Pacific Ocean in the other?

My friend, Gabby, and I are learning a piano duet. It's called "In a Persian Market." We plan to enter the talent contest that our school has every spring. If we start practicing now, we might be ready by then.

You probably won't get another letter for a while

because Mrs. Lumbard is making us write two pages about someone in our family. Nobody in my family is interesting enough to fill up two whole pages. I will have to write big.

Your pen pal,
Julie

Dear Mrs. Kaplan,

How is everything at Shady Villa? I hope your daughter brings you enchiladas again soon. I did what you said and went to the library and looked up the building of the Panama Canal.

One encyclopedia told about the engineers who built the dam, but it didn't mention your dad's name. It says the canal cost more than three hundred sixty million dollars. How much of that did your dad get? Lots, I hope.

Speaking of encyclopedias, Frankie has decided to memorize all of the topic headings in our set of encyclopedias. Can you believe it? He has been working on it for a week, and he's already halfway through Volume One. When Frankie decides to do something, he forgets everything else in the world.

His strategy is to learn the topics in groups of three, and then just keep adding to what he already knows. This project is driving me nuts. Frankie walks around muttering lists of words to himself.

Today at breakfast Mom asked him if he wanted more toast, and he replied, *"Afghan hound, Africa, African violet."*

Peg Kehret

When we got on the school bus this morning, the driver said, "Good morning, Frankie," and Frankie said, *"Alabama, Alabaster, Aladdin."*

The driver just smiled; I guess she's used to Frankie. Or maybe compared to the cuss words some kids use, the headings of the encyclopedia are a relief.

I have to quit now. Mom and Dad are making me go to bed a half hour early because I was so slow getting up this morning.

Your pen pal,
Julie

Dear Mrs. Kaplan,

Good news! I got an A on the two-page paper I wrote. I told how my mother can communicate without using words. She has these looks that she gives me and she does not have to say a single thing and I know exactly what she means.

For example, if I take the lid off the cookie jar while she is fixing dinner, she looks at me with her eyebrows slightly raised. She does not make a sound, but I know she is telling me, *Don't eat cookies now or you will spoil your appetite for dinner.*

It's okay with me if I spoil my appetite, but when the eyebrows go up, the lid on the cookie jar goes back down.

If we are out shopping and I see something really cool that costs more money than I have, like a set of twenty sparkle nail polishes, I'll take it off the shelf and show it to Mom and she'll kind of roll her eyes and shake her head. That means, *Don't even think about asking me to pay good money for that junk. Put it back right now.*

I am the only girl in my entire school who has no sparkle nail polish. Mom says it looks cheap. How can it look cheap when it costs so much?

At least I got an A on my report.

Your unsparkly pen pal,
Julie

Dear Mrs. Kaplan,

Do you have any suggestions for how a fifth-grade girl can atone for her transgressions? Isn't that a great phrase? I read it in a religious magazine when I was at my grandma's house.

I have decided I should atone for my transgressions. Maybe Mom and Dad will forgive me if I do some really great atonement, but I can't think what that would be and I don't dare ask Frankie or he'll come up with an idea that gets me into even more trouble than I'm already in, which is plenty.

As usual, it was all Frankie's fault. I *told* him we shouldn't do it, that it would scare Mom and Dad half to death, but he said, "Oh, no, it won't. They'll realize it's only a joke. They'll think it's funny."

So I helped him stuff a pair of my jeans and one of my shirts with old towels. We even stuffed the shirt-sleeves so it looked as if there were arms inside.

Frankie blew up a peach-colored balloon, and I helped him glue it to the shirt collar. I got an old brown wig out of the dress-up-clothes box, and we glued it on the balloon. We used markers to add eyes, nose, and mouth. Then we pinned my favorite base-ball cap to the wig.

Frankie stuffed washcloths into a pair of my socks, then stapled the socks to the legs of the jeans.

We propped the dummy against my dresser and stood back to admire our creation.

"It's you!" Frankie said.

I stared at the lumpy figure with its limp hair.

"This does not look one bit like me," I said. "The balloon is too pink."

"It's close enough," Frankie declared.

I took the brown marker and drew eyelashes on the balloon face. That helped a little.

"Why don't you add some mascara?" Frankie said. "How about a little perfume behind the ears?"

"Take one of those towels out of the jeans," I said. "The dummy is way too fat."

"It's you," Frankie repeated.

When I got done bopping Frankie on the head with my pillow, we dragged the dummy to my bedroom window. My room is on the second story of our house, on the back side. The house is built on a hill, so it's far-ther than a two-story drop from my window to the ground.

We looked out. Mom and Dad were sitting on the small deck that adjoins the living room, off to the left and one floor down. Both had an excellent view of the vast space between my window and the hillside below.

Frankie whispered, "As soon as we shove the dummy out, start screaming."

I peeked at my parents. They were reading the newspaper and drinking coffee.

"Maybe this isn't a good idea," I said. "They look pretty relaxed down there. If I suddenly start screaming, it's going to startle them. What if they don't realize it's a dummy? What if they think I really fell?"

"Quit worrying," Frankie said. "You said yourself the dummy doesn't look anything like you. They'll know it's a joke. Mom and Dad are going to think this is hysterical."

Hysterical. Ha! Mom and Dad were hysterical, all right, but not the way Frankie predicted.

Here is what happened: Frankie yelled, "Watch out!" Mom and Dad looked up. Then we shoved the dummy out my window. As soon as it cleared the windowsill, I started screaming at the top of my lungs. I have to admit, that part of the stunt was fun. I didn't know I could make such a racket.

While I screamed, Frankie leaned out the window, pointed at the dummy, and shrieked, "Julie! Julie!"

Mom and Dad dropped the newspapers as they leaped from their chairs. Dad's coffee spilled all over his pants. To say they looked horrified is definitely an understatement. Dad raced down the stairs from the deck to the backyard while Mom ran inside and called 911.

By the time I got downstairs, Mom had given our

address to the emergency operator and was rushing toward where the dummy lay faceup in the grass.

"Is she alive?" Mom shouted to Dad. The fear in her voice made me feel guilty. "Can she talk?"

Dad stood looking down at the dummy. "Our daughter is not injured," he said. "Yet." His voice sounded like stainless steel. "But as soon as I get my hands on her, that will change."

I raced over to them. They glared at me as if I had just murdered my brother, which at that moment I began to consider.

"It was a joke," I said. "You're supposed to be laughing."

I couldn't hear their reply because of the shrieking sirens.

The medics arrived. Frankie led them around the side of the house, pointed to Mom and Dad, and then disappeared. What a coward.

Mom and Dad were definitely not laughing as they explained to the medics that it wasn't a real body, it was only a dummy, but they *thought* it was a real body when they called for help.

The medics were not laughing as they told me how serious it is to make a prank call to the emergency number. I wanted to say, *"I* didn't make the call," but I saw the look on Dad's face and kept my mouth shut.

Our neighbors came over because they heard the ambulance and were afraid someone had broken a leg or had a heart attack. They were not laughing when they went back home.

I am not laughing, either, as I sit in my room in time-out for probably the rest of my life, with my allowance canceled and my computer privileges taken away, which is why I am writing this letter in longhand and can't check the spelling.

It really isn't fair that I always get punished for Frankie's ideas.

"You're the oldest," Mom said. "Frankie's only nine and you're eleven. You should have more sense."

Mom is always telling me stuff that I already know. I mean, my age and my brother's age are hardly big news.

Besides, I don't see that being eleven has anything to do with it. If Frankie didn't come up with wild plans, I wouldn't be able to help him, and Mom and Dad would still be speaking to me, and I would stay out of trouble.

Frankie's in time-out, too, but that doesn't help me any. If you know any good atonements, let me know right away.

An eleven-year-old transgressor,
Julie

Dear Mrs. Kaplan,

It's been awhile since I wrote because to tell you the truth I was kind of mad that you took my parents' side over the Dummy-Out-the-Window trick.

You are getting this letter now because I am in time-out again and don't have anything else to do. Also, I thought about what you said—that my parents were scared they were about to lose me forever and that's why they got so angry. Believe me, I'll never shove another dummy out a window and scream bloody murder while it falls.

The reason I am in time-out today is because Frankie got me in trouble again. You would think I would learn to ignore him, but his ideas always sound good and it isn't until the prank is over that I realize I've messed up again.

This time I've lost my allowance for two weeks because I got disqualified from the pancake toss at our church's pancake breakfast. It really was not my fault because I didn't even know about Frankie's scheme until the last minute, and then there wasn't time to think it over.

Our church has this event every year to raise money for choir robes or hymnals or something. All the women cook pancakes and sausage, and the men serve coffee and juice.

Then comes the fun part: the annual pancake toss for kids. After everyone has eaten, the cooks fry all the extra pancake batter, and they have a contest to see which kid can throw a pancake the farthest.

In case you're wondering, those pancakes don't get wasted. Not when there are starving children in Albania, to quote my mother. (Any time we have broccoli or cauliflower or some other yucky food that makes me gag, Mom reminds me of the starving children in Albania. I don't even know where Albania is.)

As I said, the pancakes don't go to waste. Mr. Zaron, who goes to our church, raises hogs, and after the pancake toss contest he gathers up all the pancakes that got thrown and takes them home for hog feed.

There are two age categories for the pancake toss: six-to-nine, and ten-to-thirteen. Frankie was in the younger category, and I was in with the older kids.

All you have to do is throw a pancake as far as you can, and the one who throws it farthest gets a prize. I almost didn't enter because my arms have been sore lately and it hurts when I throw anything, but local merchants donated some really neat prizes this year.

First prize in my age group was a gift certificate for All For Kids Bookstore. I really wanted to win it because there's a new book I want to read, and I've been on the wait list at the library for over a month already. Which is why I agreed to Frankie's suggestion.

It wasn't really cheating. No rule stated that the pancakes couldn't be frozen.

This is what happened. Right at the start of the breakfast, Frankie stuck two pancakes in the church freezer. By the time everyone ate and it was time for the pancake toss, those two pancakes were as hard as Frisbies.

The younger kids went first. Most of them could only throw their pancakes a few feet. Frankie's went way farther than the others, sliced to the right, and rolled under a parked car.

Everyone cheered, and Frankie got the first-place prize: a skateboard.

The judges backed up for the older kids. There were twelve of us, including three kids from my school: the Jersey twins, Bo-Bob and John, and Evelyn Gilmore, who drives me crazy because she's always trying to impress the grown-ups with her angelic behavior. I thought for sure one of the twins would win, since they are both pitchers on the school baseball team.

"Go last," Frankie whispered to me. Then he took off for the kitchen to get my pancake out of the freezer.

Most of the kids flung their pancakes ten or twelve feet. Bo-Bob and John threw theirs about fifteen feet, with Bo-Bob's going slightly farther than John's.

I went last. Frankie slipped me my frozen pancake, and when I threw it, it sailed right past the others, over the heads of the judges, and landed on the far side of the parking lot. The second-place pancake tosser, Bo-Bob, wasn't even close.

I collected my All For Kids certificate and stuck around to receive congratulations. Big mistake.

The mother of one of the other contestants helped retrieve the pancakes for Mr. Zaron's hogs.

"Wait a minute!" she yelled when she picked up my winning pancake. "This pancake is as hard as a rock. No wonder it went so far. It's frozen solid!"

Mom got her *I can't believe my own child would disgrace me this way* look.

A little kid who had competed in Frankie's group immediately crawled under the parked car and got Frankie's pancake and gave it to one of the judges.

"This one was frozen, too," the judge said. "It's partially thawed now, but you can see where a piece snapped off when it hit the pavement."

You never saw so many frowns and shaking heads and pointing fingers. Those people acted as if Frankie and I had stolen dollar bills from the collection plate.

"I am mortified," my mother said, "to think you

would cheat, at church of all places. This behavior is totally unacceptable."

That isn't big news; a lot of my behavior is not acceptable to my mother, but this time she said it in a way that let me know she was furious and I was in big-time trouble.

They held the pancake toss over again, and Frankie and I were disqualified. The Jersey twins had already gone home by then, so that prissy prude, Evelyn Gilmore, won for the older kids, and I had to give her my All For Kids certificate.

When she took it, she pointed to a bracelet she always wears that says "Do What's Right" on it, and she whispered to me, "Was it right to use a frozen pancake?"

She looked so smug and self-righteous that I whispered back to her, "Is it right to keep a prize that you didn't win? An unselfish person would give it to someone less fortunate, who is in trouble."

I held out my hand.

Evelyn hesitated. Another few seconds and the All For Kids gift certificate would have been mine.

But just then Dad came over and told me, "Get in the car. We are going straight home."

From the way he said it, I knew we were not going to rent movies, the way we had planned.

It is too bad that Frankie got disqualified, because he might have won even if he had not used frozen pancakes. He has a strong throwing arm. Good arm, bad ideas.

> From your pen pal
> whose behavior is totally unacceptable,
> *Julie*

P.S. Frankie is now up to the *B*'s in the encyclopedia. He is using his time-out to memorize some more. I can hear him in his room saying, *"Beeswax, Beet, Beethoven."* If I ever get my allowance back, I am going to buy earplugs.

November 1

Dear Mrs. Kaplan,

Guess what! I am running for student council! This is how it happened: I have two best friends, Sarah and Gabby. Last summer we made a pact that since this is our last year at Adams Elementary School (next year we will go to Lincoln Middle School), we would each do one really big thing during fifth grade. Something to help our school. My dad says we plan to leave in a blaze of glory.

Gabby volunteered to be in charge of the spring talent show. That's why she and I started practicing our duet so soon. If we win our school's talent show, we go to the district competition, and if we win there, we get a trophy for the Adams School trophy case that's next to the principal's office.

Sarah hasn't decided yet what she will do, but I know she'll think of something really good.

Anyway, when Mrs. Lumbard said she was taking applications for people who would be willing to run for student council, I remembered our pact, and I decided to do it.

There are eight candidates and we each had to decide on a platform and a slogan.

My platform is to clean up our school and recycle all the litter. You should see the mess in the parking lot. There are gum wrappers and empty soda cans and other litter all over the place. It's disgusting.

It's that way on the playground, too, only there most of the junk has blown up against the fence. It looks like multicolored snowdrifts.

We even get trash in Adams Fountain, which is this really nice fountain in the courtyard. It sprays water in the air. (The water is not wasted; it goes through some pipes and comes back into the fountain again.)

Our school is U-shaped, and the fountain is in the middle, at the closed end of the *U*. There are some picnic tables by it. In warm weather we get to eat lunch there, and paper napkins or sandwich bags sometimes blow into the water and no one ever fishes them out.

There is litter in the whole neighborhood around the school because kids walking to and from school unwrap candy and gum and just throw the wrappers on the sidewalk.

Some people who live near the school clean up their yards regularly, but others let the trash accumulate in their shrubs. They are probably tired of picking up junk only to have more the next day.

Anyway, my platform is that if I am elected to the student council, I'll have kids sign up to do litter pickups. We'll get recycle containers for paper and for aluminum cans, and we'll make posters to remind people where to put their trash.

I will personally make sure there's no junk in Adams Fountain.

I'm even planning to have an assembly where we learn about the things that can be made out of recycled materials. I am going to invite Mr. Irving to be the speaker. I met him when my parents made me go with them to the Home and Garden Show. Most of it was boring, but one exhibit showed all the items that can be made from recycled things.

Mr. Irving worked in that exhibit. He gave me two pencils, a blue one made from recycled jeans and a green one made out of old money. I now have pencils made from Levi's and dollar bills!

So that is my platform—to clean up the school and recycle the trash.

I have one big problem, though. I can't think of a good slogan. Mrs. Lumbard says a catchy slogan is imperative. (*Imperative* is one of our spelling words this week.)

Frankie suggested one slogan, but it is so gross I won't repeat it, even to you. It had to do with recycling slugs by turning them into garden fertilizer.

Fortunately Dad asked what Frankie planned to use the blender for *before* Frankie put the slugs in it. Otherwise I would never make blackberry milk shakes in the blender again.

Speaking of Frankie, he has offered to help me with my campaign. He says if I print up fliers, he will distribute them for me. The only catch is that I have to do dishes three times when it is his turn. Frankie hates doing dishes.

He is now on Volume Three of the encyclopedias. All he said at breakfast today was *"Cobra, Cobweb, Coca-Cola."* He can actually start at the beginning of the *A*'s and rattle off the whole thing, all the way to *Coca-Cola*. I have to admit, it's impressive.

After I hear him practice, though, I can never get the words out of my mind. You know how sometimes a song will go over and over in your head? Well, that's what happens to me with Frankie's encyclopedia headings. They just pop into my thoughts and repeat endlessly.

I wish a good slogan would pop into my thoughts.

The candidate with no slogan,

Julie

P.S. Gabby and I decided "In a Persian Market" is a boring title, so we are learning a new duet called "Boogie-Woogie Blues."

Dear Mrs. Kaplan,

You are a genius! That was the best idea I ever heard.

I might have thought of "Keep Adams Clean," but I would never have thought about blowing soap bubbles on the playground while I handed out my flyers.

Frankie blew bubbles for me, too, and so did Sarah and Gabby and Keelie.

It worked just the way you said it would. All the kids came over to chase the soap bubbles, and while they tried to pop bubbles they listened to my campaign speech. Lots of people said they will vote for me. Thank you! Thank you!

I'm still on the early bedtime even though it has not helped. I still wake up stiff and sore. I try to hurry in the mornings, but it's hard to move fast when all my joints hurt.

I told Mom that a new bedroom set with a fancy lace canopy would correct the problem, but she just gave me her look that means *Don't be ridiculous.*

I'm sorry you aren't feeling well. It must be terrible to be old and sick and not get any mail except from me. I'll try to write more often. It's good that your daughter is a nurse and that you can talk to her on the phone.

Your bubbly pen pal,
Julie

P.S. I have to go to the doctor tomorrow for a checkup. Mom made the appointment after she heard me tell Gabby I wasn't going to practice our duet because my hands were too sore. She says kids don't have growing pains in their hands. I hope I won't have to get a shot.

Dear Mrs. Kaplan,

I know I just wrote to you yesterday and I really don't have anything new to tell you, but I am at the doctor's office and there isn't anything good to read.

I checked the dates on all the magazines; the most recent one has been here for eighteen months. Mom is reading an article called "How to Flatten Your Stomach in Only Five Days." It probably doesn't matter if that one is eighteen months old.

There is a reason why these areas are called waiting rooms. I have waited and waited and waited.

First I got checked by my regular doctor. He was only ten minutes late, but he asked me about a million questions. He seemed particularly interested in the fact that I am always stiff and sore when I first get up in the morning. He kept feeling my elbows while I moved my arms, and then he felt my knees while I swung my legs back and forth. It was pretty boring.

Then he said he wanted to run a few tests, starting with a blood test. I told him my blood doesn't hurt at all, it's my arms and legs and hands, but he sent me two floors down to the lab anyway.

When I got there, a nurse asked for a urine sample. I will say no more about that.

I waited some more and then the nurse poked a needle in my arm and withdrew a whole bottle full of my blood. Not a big milk bottle, just a small bottle, but still it wasn't much fun to watch that empty container fill up with red fluid and know that it was all coming out of my veins.

If I cut myself tonight, I won't even need a bandage. There isn't anything left inside me to ooze out.

When the blood ordeal was over, I thought I would finally get to go home, but, no, here I am in another waiting room. This time they are going to take X-rays of my hands.

Mom promised it won't hurt, and I know she's right because I got my teeth X-rayed at the dentist once, and I didn't even feel it, but I am getting nervous about all these tests. The doctors don't X-ray your hands and withdraw all your blood if they suspect you have dandruff. I just hope

Later:

I quit writing because it was my turn for the X-rays. When they were over, we finally got to leave.

Mom stopped at Dairy Queen on the way home and let me order a banana split, which is rare. Usually I only get a cone because too much sugar will rot my teeth, not to mention spoil my appetite for dinner.

Peg Kehret

Mom said the banana split was a reward for being so good about all the tests. She rewarded herself with a banana split, too, which probably won't help the flat stomach project any, but I didn't say that.

Do they ever serve banana splits at Shady Villa?

Your bloodless friend,
Julie

November 11

Dear Mrs. Kaplan,

Last night I got in trouble for staying up too late when I was supposed to be asleep. I don't need to tell you whose fault it was.

Frankie and I used to go to bed at 8:30 on school nights, but I am tired a lot (one reason I had to go to the doctor), so now I have to be in bed at eight o'clock. I'm the oldest and I have to go to bed first! Talk about unfair.

Anyway, last night I was in bed on time, but I couldn't go to sleep because I could hear Frankie saying, over and over, *"Cow, Cowbird, Cowboy."*

He says when the headings are alike, they are harder to memorize than when they are different. After the seventh time of hearing, *"Cow, Cowbird, Cowboy,"* I couldn't stand it. I got out of bed and went into Frankie's room.

"What in the world is a cowbird?" I asked. I thought for sure he was making that one up.

But, no. It seems there really is a cowbird. It's a member of the blackbird family. Frankie showed me the heading in the encyclopedia, and I started to read, and the cowbird is so interesting that I read the whole section.

Here is what I learned: The female cowbird does not build a nest of her own. Instead, she lays her egg in the nest of some unsuspecting bird of a different species. The other bird hatches the cowbird's egg along with her own.

That's right. While the other mother bird sits on all the eggs, the mother cowbird is flying off wherever she wants to go. (She is free as a bird! Ha ha.)

As if that is not bad enough, when the eggs hatch, the baby cowbirds are big and greedy and usually manage to get most of the food that's meant for the other baby birds. Sometimes the young cowbirds even push the smaller birds out of the nest!

Then when the cowbird grows up, it leaves its foster parents and flies off to join a flock of cowbirds. As far as I could tell, the foster mother bird gets nothing for her time.

If I had not read all of this with my own eyes, I would never have believed it.

Unfortunately, Frankie and I were still discussing cowbirds at ten o'clock when Dad poked his head in the door. That's when we got in trouble for not being asleep. I told Dad we were learning about birds, but he said we can improve our education prior to eight o'clock at night.

How can anyone sleep when a voice in the next room keeps saying, *"Cow, Cowbird, Cowboy,"* over and over?

Signed: Sleepless

November 13

Dear Mrs. Kaplan,

   The most terrible, horrible thing in the whole world has happened. For once, it isn't Frankie's fault.

   I am too upset to write any more.

                              Your unhappy pen pal,
                              Julie

November 17

Dear Mrs. Kaplan,

It was nice of you to call. I'm sorry that my letter worried you, and I'm sorry we weren't home so you had to talk to Stupid But Essential.

That's what Mom calls our answering machine: Stupid But Essential. She hates it when a machine answers, but she admits it's handy to be able to leave a message and not have to keep calling back until someone is home.

When we've been gone, Mom always goes in the house and says, "Hi, Stupid But Essential. Did anyone call?" Then she pushes the little button and Stupid But Essential replies.

I would have called you back only you did not leave a number.

Or if you did, Stupid But Essential forgot to tell us.

Anyway, the horrible thing that happened is that I found out why my joints hurt all the time and why it's hard for me to get moving in the morning. Mom and Dad and I went back to Dr. Stephens to get the results of all those tests. I didn't really know what to expect, but I did NOT expect what happened.

32

He had us all sit down in his office, and he told us that I have arthritis! The same as you. Well, not exactly the same as you. What I have is juvenile rheumatoid arthritis, and I am plenty bummed out about it.

I still can hardly believe it. I always thought arthritis was something old people got. When you told me you have arthritis in your hands, I didn't give it a second thought. People who are eighty-nine years old *expect* to have arthritis. People who are eleven years old expect to get colds or the flu or maybe a broken arm. But arthritis? No way.

From now on, my doctor will be Dr. McLean because he specializes in JRA. (That's how they abbreviate Juvenile Rheumatoid Arthritis.) He explained that my legs and shoulders ache because the joints are swollen. Same with my hands.

Dr. McLean said the reason I'm hurting so much right now is that I'm having what he called a flare. I am not kidding. When my joints get swollen, it's called a flare. It sounds as if I'm part of a Fourth of July display.

The opposite of a flare is what Dr. McLean calls a nonactive phase. That means the JRA goes away for a while. Sometimes nonactive phases last only a few weeks, and sometimes the JRA never comes back.

The worst part is this: there isn't any cure! I'm taking some pills so my joints won't hurt so much, but the bottom line is, I have to live with this dumb disease unless I get lucky and it goes away on its own. If that does not happen, the best I can hope for is that I'll have some long nonactive times in between flares.

That isn't all. There could be complications such as problems with my eyes. So far that has not happened, thank goodness.

I haven't told any of my friends yet. I'm not sure what to say. I wish I had an exciting disease that everyone would be sympathetic over. But arthritis? Yuck.

Dr. McLean gave us some pamphlets to read and one for me to give to my teacher. I did not want to take it to Mrs. Lumbard, but Mom and Dad made me.

Your JRA friend,

Julie

P.S. I forgot to tell you what Frankie said when he learned I have arthritis. Now, you would expect a loving little brother to say something like "That's too bad," or "Oh, no!" or even just "Rats!"

What did Frankie say? He said, *"Arthritis* comes between *artesian well* and *arthropod."* As if I cared what is on either side of *arthritis* in the encyclopedia. By the way, he just started Volume Four.

November 22

Dear Mrs. Kaplan,

Can you believe that a poor unfortunate child with JRA whose legs hurt so much she can't roller-skate is in time-out? Well, I am.

As usual, it was Frankie's idea.

Last night Mom asked if my friends were curious about JRA. I admitted I had not told anyone. Dad said I had to tell my friends what was wrong with me because it's worse to pretend that everything is okay. I said I didn't want to tell them.

Frankie took my side. He came into my room while I was supposed to be doing my homework but was really reading my *American Girl* magazine.

He said, "Mom and Dad are wrong. If you tell everyone you have arthritis, they're going to laugh and say, 'Oh, my grandma has arthritis.' Kids will call you Granny Julie."

"I know that," I said, "and you know that, but Mom and Dad don't know that. They made me promise I would tell my friends that I have JRA."

Frankie looked thoughtful. "I agree you have to tell your friends you have a disease," he said. "You don't do a lot of stuff that you used to do, such as roller-skate, and it's better for your friends to know you have a disease than to have them think you're lazy or that you just don't want to play when they ask you.

"Besides, you missed two days of school to go to doctors and now you get excused from class to take medicine every afternoon, so your friends already know something is wrong."

"But . . ."

"But you don't have to tell them what's really wrong. As long as you have to have a disease, why not have something exotic?"

"Like what?"

"Like typhoid fever."

"I think you have to be in a jungle to get typhoid fever."

"You'll think of something," Frankie said.

And I did.

When I got to school this morning, Sarah and Gabby were waiting for me, as usual, next to the fountain.

"The doctor says I have a disease," I told them.

"Do you have to have an operation?" Gabby asked.

"No," I said. "At least not now."

"Is it serious?" Sarah said.

"I'm going to tell you because you're my two best friends," I said, "but you have to promise not to tell anyone else."

Sarah looked worried. "Is it something really bad?" she said.

"Promise you won't tell?"

Sarah nodded. So did Gabby.

"Say it out loud," I said. "Say, 'I promise not to tell anyone what's wrong with Julie.' "

They both repeated the promise.

I whispered in Sarah's ear.

"Oh, no," she said.

"What? What?" said Gabby.

I whispered in Gabby's ear.

"Are you going to die?" Gabby asked.

"Everyone dies some time," I said.

"Oh, Julie, you're so brave," Sarah said. "If I had—" she paused. "If I had what you have," she continued, "I don't think I'd be able to come to school at all."

The bell rang and we hurried into our classroom.

The rest of the day was great. Sarah offered to carry my library books for me when we had library hour. Carrying anything heavy always makes my shoulders ache, so I let her do that. Gabby gave me one of her Twinkies at lunch, without my even offering to trade for it.

"If you're giving away Twinkies, I'll take one," Keelie said.

Gabby answered, "Only to Julie. She's quite sick, you know."

"And you think Twinkies will make her better?" Keelie said.

"She doesn't look sick," Evelyn said.

"Sometimes the worst illnesses are the ones that don't show," Sarah said. Her voice got all quivery. She jumped up, threw her milk carton in the garbage can, and rushed out of the cafeteria.

I tried to look tragic.

After that, Keelie offered to scrape my lunch tray for me, and Evelyn asked if she could sit next to me in music class.

I decided having JRA isn't so bad, after all.

When I got home from school, my mother said, "Did you tell the other kids what the doctors said?"

"I talked to Gabby and Sarah," I said, "but I asked them not to tell anyone because I don't want everyone to feel sorry for me."

Tears sprang to Mom's eyes. "I'm so proud of you," she said. "You are taking this like a real trooper."

A couple of hours later I was in the bathroom practicing my tragic look in front of the mirror when the doorbell rang.

"Julie!" Mom called. "Sarah's here."

I started toward the front hall.

I heard Mrs. Borden, Sarah's mother, say, "I brought a casserole and a lemon pie for your dinner." Then she burst into tears.

I had a sudden, sinking feeling that Sarah had not kept her promise.

Mom took Mrs. Borden's arm and led her into the

kitchen. Mrs. Borden put the casserole on the table. Sarah, who was trailing behind her mother and refusing to look at me, put the lemon pie next to it.

"I'm sorry," Mrs. Borden said. "I didn't think I'd lose control this way. Sarah told me about Julie's diagnosis, and I'm so terribly sorry."

"It's kind of you to be concerned," Mom said, "but it isn't the end of the world. We'll cope."

"I don't know how you can be so calm," Mrs. Borden said. "I took the liberty of putting Julie's name on the prayer chain at my church. I knew you wouldn't mind."

I glared at Sarah, my ex–best friend.

"Isn't the prayer chain usually for critically ill people?" Mom said.

Mrs. Borden wiped her eyes. "It doesn't get much more critical than a brain tumor," she said.

"Traitor!" I hissed at Sarah.

"I couldn't help it," she said. "Mom *made* me tell."

"Brain tumor!" Mom said. "Who has a brain tumor?"

"Julie does," Mrs. Borden said. "Doesn't she?"

Mom gave me her special look that means, *I won't yell at you in front of company, but just wait until they leave.*

Mrs. Borden said, "Sarah came home from school and flopped on her bed, sobbing her eyes out, and refused to tell me what was wrong."

"I don't want you to die," Sarah said.

Mrs. Borden continued, "When I finally threatened to make Sarah stay home from Keelie's overnight party, she told me that Julie has a brain tumor."

"Julie does not have a brain tumor," Mom said. "She has juvenile rheumatoid arthritis."

"Arthritis?" Sarah squeaked. "Like Great-grandma?"

"You see?" I said to Mom. "You see why I had to do it?"

What happened next was not pretty.

Mom told Mrs. Borden she could keep the casserole and the pie.

Mrs. Borden looked at me as if I was covered with scum.

Sarah said, "I cried for over an hour and made my eyes red and my nose all stuffed up, and all you have is arthritis, which is hardly worth crying about."

That's when *I* burst into tears, surprising even myself. "That just shows how much you know," I cried. "My disease may not have a scary name, but my legs hurt all the time and my shoulders hurt and I can't roller-skate anymore or get things down from the top shelf. My hands throb when I practice my piano lessons, and I can barely drag myself out of bed every day because I ache all over, and there isn't any cure, and I don't want to have arthritis and be different from everybody else."

I sank into one of the kitchen chairs, put my head down on the table, and bawled.

For a few seconds nobody spoke.

Then Sarah said, "Can't you get a shot or something, to make you well? Or go to a different doctor?"

I shook my head, trying to quit crying.

Mom handed me a tissue.

"Julie's doctor is a highly respected specialist," Mom said. "He says there is no cure for JRA."

Sarah started to cry, too. "Is Julie going to die?"

"JRA is not fatal," Mom said softly, "but it is chronic, which means Julie will have this for a long time. She takes a medication to reduce the swelling and another to make her more comfortable."

"There are a bunch of side effects like upset stomach and a skin rash," I said.

"That may not happen," Mom said. "Those are only possible side effects."

Mrs. Borden said, "I'm so sorry, Julie, that you have juvenile rheumatoid arthritis. I don't blame you for being upset. I hope my casserole and lemon pie will taste good."

"I'm sorry you got a chronic disease," Sarah said. "I wish your legs didn't hurt."

"It's always best to tell the truth," Mom said, as if I had not just figured that out for myself.

"I was so scared," Sarah said. "I thought you were going to die."

She looked so miserable that I decided to forgive her for blabbing my secret. It was kind of nice to know she had cried so hard over me. Also, she had remembered that lemon pie is my favorite.

After Sarah and Mrs. Borden left, Mom said it is a disgrace to lie to my friends. She made me call Gabby and tell her that I don't have a brain tumor, I have JRA. Gabby sounded relieved, but I bet she won't give me her Twinkie tomorrow.

Then Mom said I need to sit in time-out and think about all of the people in Mrs. Borden's church who are now praying for me to be healed from a brain tumor. I tried to think about them, but I don't know who they are, so I wrote this letter to you instead.

I asked Mom if I could take a piece of lemon pie into time-out with me. She did not even bother to answer. She just gave me her look that means *You are wasting your breath to ask that, but I won't waste my breath replying.*

If there are mistakes in this letter or my writing seems wobbly, it's because Itty Bitty Kitty keeps sitting on the page while I write. She thinks she is a paperweight.

Your disgraced friend,
Julie

November 25

Dear Mrs. Kaplan,

Gabby was really nice about the slight difference between my having a brain tumor and my having JRA. She says we can put off practicing "Boogie-Woogie Blues" until my hands aren't so sore. The talent show isn't for five months, so we'll still have plenty of time.

I wish I didn't have to take so much medicine. It doesn't taste too bad, but I take it four times a day, which means I have to take one dose at school every day. I get excused from class, go to the nurse's office, and she gives me a little spoonful of medicine. It's embarrassing.

I don't see why I can't just carry the bottle and a spoon in my lunch bag every day, and then during afternoon recess I could go in the rest room and swallow the medicine. But, no, it has to be a big deal with me getting excused from class.

I also take pills twice a day, but I get those at breakfast and before I go to bed, so they aren't a problem.

Sarah found her special project. She's going to be in charge of a Fun Run to raise money for some new playground equipment. Kids sign up to be in the run, and then they get people to sponsor them, which means the people pay money if the kid finishes the race, and all the money goes to Adams School.

The Fun Run is four miles long, and Sarah hopes to have every single kid in school enter it. The race will be next April, so everyone has lots of time to talk their relatives into being a sponsor.

It sounds like a good project, but one thing worries me. My legs hurt if I run very far. I'm afraid I might not be able to finish the race. If I drop out partway through, would my sponsors still have to pay?

Happy Thanksgiving!

Julie

November 28

Dear Mrs. Kaplan,

I just realized something. I write to you when I need to talk to someone and don't know who to talk to. I hope you don't mind. At the start of this project I told you I am not a good letter-writer, and here I am sending you a letter practically every week. You can pretend they are junk mail and throw them away without opening them if you get sick of hearing from me.

There is a sign hanging in our kitchen: NO WHINING. It has been there forever. Sometimes if Frankie or I complain about something, Mom points to the sign. Another example of her nonverbal communication. Too bad I forgot to put that in the paper I wrote. Maybe I would have gotten an A+ instead of an A.

Mom has pointed at the sign a lot lately but I don't think I have been whining. So I am writing to you to get your opinion.

Is it whining to say:

1. My backpack is too heavy. My shoulders ache from carrying it back and forth to school.
2. It isn't fair that Evelyn Gilmore got her pic-

ture in the paper for being a candidate for student council.

3. How come we never have chocolate-chip cookies for dessert?

I bet if our house was on fire and I told Mom it was too hot in here, she would point to the NO WHINING sign and keep right on doing whatever she was doing.

One reason I like Itty Bitty Kitty so much is that she does not care if I whine. As long as I rub behind her ears while I'm talking, I can say anything I want and she just purrs and digs her front claws in and out of my jeans.

A cat's life is so uncomplicated. No mother cat pointing her paw at a NO WHINING sign. No medicine to swallow, except once when she got worms. No little brother babbling, *"Deer, Deer Fly, Deer Mouse."*

Most of all, no JRA.

Your friend who has plenty to whine about,

Julie

December 2

Dear Mrs. Kaplan,

We did the soap bubbles during lunch recess again today, and they were even more of a hit this time. Some kids have started calling me The Bubble Girl. Sarah and Gabby made some signs that say KEEP ADAMS CLEAN. VOTE FOR THE BUBBLE GIRL.

I think I actually have a chance of winning. At least my campaign is fun, which is more than I can say for Evelyn Gilmore's. Her slogan is "Honesty, Integrity, and Principle." Talk about boring. Not only boring, but some of the kids who can't spell think *principle* means Mr. Randolph.

I always know the correct spelling because my second-grade teacher taught me a trick: "The principal is your pal." If you remember that, you know to end it *p-a-l*.

Evelyn came over to me today while I was blowing bubbles and said, "Be careful not to spill your bubble solution. It's very slippery and someone might get hurt." Gag. I felt like pouring it on her head, but I controlled myself.

I don't have to get excused from class and go to the nurse's office to take my medicine anymore.

Here is what happened: On Monday during afternoon recess I went into the nurse's office and said, "Since I was going past, I decided to come in and take my medicine."

It was only twenty minutes before the scheduled time, so she gave it to me.

I did the same thing on Tuesday.

When I showed up again on Wednesday, the nurse said, "Would you prefer to come in for your medicine during recess every day instead of being called out of class?"

"Yes," I said. "It's embarrassing to be excused every day."

She nodded. "It makes too big a deal out of the medication. Right?"

"Right. I don't see why I can't just bring the bottle in my lunch and then take some during recess."

"State law prohibits that," the nurse said. "But any time you want to stop in during recess, it's okay with me."

So now I just go in every day and swallow my medicine.

> Your bubbly friend who just might get elected to student council, thanks to you,
> *Julie*

P.S. Itty Bitty Kitty is in cat time-out. She climbed the drapes.

December 10

Dear Mrs. Kaplan,

Are you okay? I've written to you three times since you last wrote back. Not that I expect a reply every time I write, but I do look forward to your letters. You always have good ideas and good advice.

I had another checkup with Dr. McLean (waiting time: twenty-seven minutes). I was not scheduled to go until next month, but my fingers are so stiff I can't play "Boogie-Woogie Blues" and I keep dropping my pencil and spilling my juice, so Mom made me go in early.

Dr. McLean sent me to an occupational therapist. He says there are some exercises that will help me stay flexible.

I don't mind doing exercises, but I was not thrilled about another waiting room. This one had coffee and tea. Why don't they have hot chocolate or maybe lemonade? Kids get thirsty, too, you know.

It's a good thing Mom doesn't read my letters. She would be pointing at the NO WHINING sign right now.

Tomorrow is the day we vote for student council representatives. Sarah, Gabby, Keelie, and I are going to get to school half an hour early and be blowing bubbles as the kids get off the school buses.

Frankie's coming, too, but I'm a little nervous about that because he says he has a wonderful surprise for me. I don't trust him. How can you trust someone who goes around mumbling, *"Dik-Dik, Dike, Dill"*?

Wish me luck tomorrow!

The hopeful candidate,
Julie

P.S. In case you are wondering, a *dik-dik* is a dwarf antelope. It's only fourteen inches high at the shoulder. I read about dik-diks after listening to Frankie practice. I'll say one thing for his project: I'm learning a lot. If the school ever gives tests on cowbirds or dik-diks, I'll be ready.

December 11

Dear Mrs. Kaplan,

I am writing this in the principal's office while I wait for Mr. Randolph to get back from a meeting. He is going to speak to me about the fact that when the teachers arrived at school this morning, they found Adams Fountain full of soap bubbles.

Someone poured dishwashing detergent in the fountain sometime last night, and when the fountain came on this morning (it's on a timer, so it comes on automatically) the motion of the water created thousands of bubbles.

By the time I got to school, the bubbles had overflowed the fountain and were halfway down the sidewalk to the street. When the school buses pulled up, all the kids cheered, "Yah! Bubble Girl!" and started stomping on the bubbles.

It got pretty wild for a while, and then a first grader slipped and fell and went crying to the nurse's office, and Evelyn Gilmore said, "I *told* you that stuff is slippery."

I think she went inside and told Mrs. Lumbard that a little kid got hurt, because first thing I knew Mrs.

Lumbard hurried out to the fountain and said, "A prank like this is not going to get you elected," and marched me down to the principal's office.

So here I sit wondering if I should tell Mr. Randolph that I didn't do it, which I didn't. The trouble is, I'm pretty sure I know who did. Remember the wonderful surprise Frankie promised me?

I have to admit it was fun and probably got me some votes, so I don't want to tattle on Frankie. But what if Mr. Randolph says I am disqualified from the election because of this, the way I got disqualified from the church pancake toss?

Oh! I hear Mr. Randolph talking to someone in the hall. Here he comes.

Later—

Mr. Randolph really is a pal. He didn't disqualify me.

He said, "Did you put the bubble solution in the fountain?"

I said, "No."

He said, "Do you know who did?"

I said, "I think so."

He said, "Do you want to tell me who it was?"

I shook my head, no.

He said, "I don't blame you. Whoever did it was only trying to help you get elected, and there wasn't any harm done."

"What about the little boy who fell?" I asked. "Is he okay?"

"Only a skinned knee. We didn't have to call his parents."

"Then I'm not in trouble?" I asked.

"No. I hope you win the election. It's high time we got rid of the litter and took some pride in our school's appearance."

Then he shook my hand and told me I could go back to class. Isn't that amazing? I always thought if you got sent to the principal's office, it meant a phone call to your parents and a black mark on your school record forever. All I got was a handshake.

Your relieved friend,

Julie

P.S. Your last letter was the best one yet. My class found Kenya on a map of Africa. We are glad you used a camera, not a gun, to shoot the elephants.

December 13

Dear Mrs. Kaplan,

I won!

I am now a fifth-grade representative to the Adams School Student Council. I got the most votes of anyone, including two votes from kids who couldn't remember my name so they wrote in "The Bubble Girl."

I know I am supposed to be a gracious winner, so I wouldn't say this to anyone around here, but you might like to know that Evelyn Gilmore came in last with only thirteen votes.

My first student council meeting is the Thursday after Winter Break. I can hardly wait.

Tonight I'm taking Sarah, Gabby, Keelie, and Frankie out for ice cream to thank them for helping me with my campaign. Dad is going to drive us. If you lived closer, I would bring you some ice cream, too. No, I wouldn't. I would bring you a cheese enchilada.

Julie Welsh
Adams School Student Council

P.S. Doesn't that look great? I may sign all my letters that way from now on.

December 19

Dear Mrs. Kaplan,

There's no school for two whole weeks. I have three new books to read during vacation.

Every day I have to do exercises that the occupational therapist taught me. The exercises are supposed to keep my joints mobile, which is good, but it hurts to do them. I soak in a hot tub first, but the exercises hurt all the same.

I told Mom, "It does not make sense to do exercises that hurt in order to keep my joints from hurting."

She has a new look that means *No excuses. Just do the exercises.*

Frankie is now on the *G*'s. I never realized how many big companies use the word *general* in their name. *General Dynamics, General Electric, General Foods, General Mills, General Motors.* It goes on and on. Wouldn't you think they could be more original?

I took your suggestion and asked the physical therapist why they provide coffee for the adults but nothing for the kids.

She said, "I never thought of that. Maybe we can get some of those juice packs."

Dad says, "Ask and ye shall receive."

I say, "Sometimes it pays to whine."

Mom and Dad moved my bedroom downstairs because climbing stairs makes my legs hurt. The den that we had the computer in is now my bedroom, and the computer is upstairs.

I didn't want to change because the downstairs room is smaller, but now that I'm here I like it because I can read in bed after everyone else has gone upstairs and nobody sees the light shining out from under my door.

Also, I can no longer hear Frankie recite the encyclopedia headings all the time.

Another good thing is that I get to sleep in my sleeping bag every night because it keeps me warmer. When my body stays warm, my joints don't stiffen up so much. Eventually I'll get a water bed or an electric mattress pad, but for now I use my sleeping bag, which means I don't have to make my bed every morning. Between the hot bath and the exercises, I have enough to do in the mornings.

I was glad to hear that carolers came to sing for you. If you lived close enough, Gabby and I would come and play "Boogie-Woogie Blues" for you.

C U L8TER,

Julie

December 24

Dear Mrs. Kaplan,

Why do the days right before Christmas go slower than other days?

I don't have any news. I'm writing to you because I don't have anything else to do.

Dad says, "No news is good news."

I say, "No news means your life is boring."

On Saturday my parents took Frankie and me to the mall to see Santa. We have been getting our pictures taken with Santa every year since we were babies. When we complain that we are too old, Dad says, "You're never too old for Santa."

Santa asked me what I want for Christmas. I told him, "I want my arthritis to go away." He looked surprised.

Frankie is spending all his time during Winter Break working on the encyclopedia. Right now he is saying, *"Iron, Iron Curtain, Iron Lung."* I don't like it when consecutive headings start with the same word. The worst was *Ham*. Did you know there are three encyclopedia headings for *Ham?* At least *Ham, Ham, Ham* was easy to memorize.

I hope you like the present I sent you.

Mussed clothes (ha, ha),

Julie

P.S. Since I started this letter, it got more exciting around here. My grandparents are visiting us, and I overheard Nana and Mom talking about me. Nobody has figured out yet that with my bedroom downstairs, I can stand just inside my door and hear most of what gets said in the kitchen.

Nana said, "How much medicine does Julie take every day?"

"The prescription medicine, to reduce the swelling, is twice a day," Mom said. "But she also takes a liquid painkiller four times a day."

"I don't see that it's helping her any," Nana said.

"Dr. McLean told us that it could take about eight weeks for Julie to notice any improvement."

"Eight weeks!" Nana said. "Do you think you should get a second opinion?"

"Dr. McLean is a pediatric rheumatologist," Mom said. "He has treated kids with JRA for over fifteen years, and I'm confident he is doing all that can be done to help Julie."

"Have you tried having her wear a copper bracelet?" Nana asked.

"No," Mom said. I could tell she was annoyed but Nana kept right on.

"What about magnets? I've heard that wearing magnets on your body can reduce the pain."

I missed the next part of the conversation because I got to thinking about taping little magnets to my knees and elbows and my ankles and my shoulders. It doesn't sound very comfortable.

When I tuned back in to what was being said in the kitchen, I heard Mom say, "I know you mean well, Mother, but we trust Julie's doctor and we're going to follow his advice."

"I just don't like seeing a child that young take so much medication," Nana said.

I was on Nana's side there. Sometimes I think my stomach will fill up with medicine and I won't have room for the good stuff, like Twinkies and jelly beans.

They stopped talking about me then and started talking about boring adult stuff like recipes, so I quit listening and lay on my bed with Itty Bitty Kitty. I have never heard Mom and Nana disagree before. It makes me unhappy, and I wish I wasn't the reason for it.

Dear Mrs. Kaplan,

I am about to tell you the most gross thing you ever heard, so if you have a weak stomach, you can quit reading now.

We've been finding big black ants in and around our house. Dad says they might be carpenter ants.

Twice I found one in my bedroom, and both times I picked it up in a tissue and flushed it down the toilet.

Yesterday I wore my favorite jeans. Last night when I got ready for bed (still eight o'clock; still unfair), my jeans were not dirty, so I laid them on my dresser. When I got up this morning, I put them on.

I was in the kitchen pouring some orange juice when I felt something crawling on my leg, *inside* my jeans. Without thinking, I smacked my hand on my leg.

Even though it was morning and I was stiff and sore, I got those jeans off in a hurry, and—you guessed it—one of those big black ants dropped out. Yuck.

Unfortunately Frankie came into the kitchen in time to watch all of the above. He yelled upstairs to Mom and Dad, "Julie has ants in her pants!"

But this is the worst part: After I threw the dead ant in the garbage and put my jeans back on, I felt something wet on my leg so I took the jeans off again, and there was squashed ant all over the inside of my jeans. *And* it was on my leg.

Double yuck! Triple yuck! Infinity yuck!

The only good part of this is that Frankie laughed so hard he forgot about reciting the headings of the encyclopedia to me while he ate his toast.

Your grossed-out friend,
Julie

P.S. My first student council meeting was fun.

Dear Mrs. Kaplan,

My fingers are not so stiff anymore, so Gabby and I are practicing "Boogie-Woogie Blues" again. I play the top notes and she plays the bottom notes. We are getting pretty good. Yesterday we only messed up four times.

Adams School has never won the district talent competition. Wouldn't it be great if Gabby and I are the ones to do it first? I've never won any kind of award. I'm sort of an average girl. The talent contest is the only chance I'll have to win a trophy for the school's trophy case. I am going to practice my half of the duet every day, even if I can't get together with Gabby.

Dr. McLean doesn't know if the medication helped my fingers or if the exercises have helped or if my JRA is just not active now.

For the last two weeks I have taken the medicine every twelve hours instead of four times a day. Now I get to quit altogether to see what happens.

Your hopeful friend,
Julie

P.S. Shouldn't a highly respected specialist be able to tell if the medicine is helping a JRA kid or not?

Dear Mrs. Kaplan,

At the student council meeting yesterday, Mr. Randolph helped me call Mr. Irving from the Home and Garden Show to ask if he'll come and talk at an assembly. It took three phone calls (press 1, press 2), but we finally reached him.

Mr. Irving said he'll come, AND he's going to bring enough pencils made from old jeans and old money so that every kid gets one! He and Mr. Randolph set the assembly for March 20. I wish it could be sooner.

Tomorrow I'm going to pass out sign-up sheets for kids who want to help with our first litter pickup. It's from eight to ten on Saturday morning.

Sarah helped me make the sign-up sheets. They say KEEP ADAMS CLEAN! We drew circles, like soap bubbles, all around the slogan. I hope a lot of people sign up.

I am almost finished with one week of no medicine. So far my joints don't seem any worse, so maybe the JRA has quit for now. Wouldn't that be great?

No pills, no ills,

Julie

Dear Mrs. Kaplan,

Twelve kids signed up for my first litter pickup, and all but one of them showed up Saturday morning. The city garbage collection company gave us some recycle bins to use. One is for aluminum cans, one for newspapers, and one for mixed paper. If there's extra mixed paper, we're supposed to put it in a brown paper bag.

The garbage company will empty the bins once a week. We filled the mixed-paper bin (plus four bags), and we filled the bin for cans, even though we stomped on all the cans to flatten them.

Two people who live across the street from the school brought over a big plate of ginger cookies for the workers. They said they wanted to thank us.

We didn't have time to finish the whole neighborhood, but we got all the stuff that had blown against the fence. Adams School looks one hundred percent better.

Mrs. Lumbard says we are supposed to ask our pen pals about their lives instead of just blabbing on about ours. Every week she will give us a question that we can ask. The next time you write, please tell me about the most interesting person you ever met. Thank you.

Your litter-free friend,

Julie

February 4

Dear Mrs. Kaplan,

You are the best pen pal of the whole fifth grade. Other people get ordinary answers to their questions, but not me! First I got to tell about the Isthmus of Panama and how much it cost to build the Canal. Next I got to tell about your camera safaris in Kenya and your log cabin in Alaska. Yesterday I got the letter about your grandmother's friend, Fanny Crosby, who wrote more than six thousand hymns even though she was blind.

Some kids said, "No way! Nobody could write that many songs, especially if she couldn't see."

Mrs. Lumbard divided our class into groups and had some kids get on the Internet and others go to the library to look in all the research books to see if we could find a hymn writer named Fanny Crosby.

I was in the Internet group, and we found her! She was blind from the time she was six weeks old. She went to school at the New York Institution for the Blind and married a blind organist. But I guess you already know all of that, since she was your grandmother's friend.

The kids doing book research found a list of the best-known hymns that Fanny Crosby wrote, and some kids knew them. Evelyn Gilmore sang one called "Blessed Assurance" to the class. She isn't the best singer in the world, but I recognized the song. We sing it in church sometimes.

The best thing we learned was that Fanny didn't write six thousand hymns, as you thought. She wrote nine thousand!

We all got so interested in Fanny Crosby that we asked if we could stay in from recess to try to learn more. Mrs. Lumbard said to tell you thank you for your letter.

From a Fanny Crosby fan,
Julie

P.S. One thing bothers me. In the *Encyclopedia Americana* it says that the reason Fanny Crosby went blind was "faulty medical advice." In other words, the doctor goofed.

That makes me plenty nervous. What if Dr. McLean goofed and I don't have JRA after all, I have something else?

February 8

Dear Mrs. Kaplan,

I told Mom about Fanny going blind. Mom said faulty medical advice was way more common in 1820, when Fanny was a baby, than it is now. She said Dr. McLean is a specialist in JRA and that I should quit worrying so much.

I have a question, but you don't have to answer it if you don't want to. Mom says I am too nosy for my own good. I prefer to think I am curious. Besides, Mrs. Lumbard said we are supposed to ask questions.

Anyway, here is my question: Since you traveled all over the world, isn't it hard now to be stuck in a place like Shady Villa? It doesn't seem fair.

Then again, if there's one thing I've learned from having JRA, it's that life isn't always fair.

Dad says, "Play the hand you're dealt."

I say, "If the cards stink, declare a misdeal."

Curious *Julie*

February 20

Dear Mrs. Kaplan,

I'm sorry it's been awhile since I wrote. I got really busy. Student council takes more time than I thought. Besides my own project of keeping the litter picked up, I have to go to meetings and help the other council members with their projects.

Yesterday we had a meeting about the school lunches. Two parents had complained that the cafeteria lunches are not nutritious. They said the meals are high in fat and we don't get enough fruits and vegetables.

I agree with the fruit part, but I don't care if they leave off the vegetables, except for corn and tomatoes. Personally, I'd like to see Twinkies for dessert now and then, but I did not say that at the meeting.

The parents had a list of foods they wanted, and the student council reps just had to listen and say if we thought kids would eat those foods or not. We all voted no on cauliflower, broccoli, and spinach, and yes on apples, bananas, and bean burritos.

The meeting ended when Mr. Randolph and the school dietitian agreed to have apples and bananas available every day, and to serve bean burritos instead of hot dogs once a month.

Gabby and I made it all the way through "Boogie-Woogie Blues" yesterday without a single mistake. By April we should be so perfect we'll get a standing ovation.

Frankie has not got me in any trouble lately. He spends all of his time memorizing the encyclopedia.

Sarah came over yesterday. She said, "Hi, Frankie," and he said, *"Kangaroo, Kangaroo Court, Kangaroo Rat."*

Sarah said Frankie is weird, so I asked him to start at the beginning and recite the headings as far as he could go. When he did, from *A* all the way to *Kangaroo Rat,* Sarah said, "That is the most amazing thing I ever heard."

What was really amazing was that I could recite most of it with him. I listen to him practice so much that I am learning the headings of the encyclopedia, too.

Sarah brought over a big stack of sponsor sheets for the Fun Run. They have a column for the kid's name, the sponsor's name, how much per mile they will pay, and the total.

At the top there's a picture of a whole bunch of runners crossing a finish line. Sarah and I are coloring in the pictures with colored pencils because the computer she used only prints in black and white.

When we got tired of coloring, we sang a hymn that Fanny Crosby wrote. Sarah said her pastor's sermon was even more boring than usual last Sunday, so she decided to look in the hymnal for Fanny Crosby's name, and there it was!

She asked the church secretary if she could make a copy of that hymn, and she brought the copy over to my house. I played the melody on the piano and we sang it.

It wasn't the most exciting song I ever heard, but after the first few thousand hymns it probably got hard for Fanny to keep thinking up new ideas. Maybe tomorrow I'll sing it for Evelyn Gilmore.

Your friend,
Julie

P.S. My JRA has not gone away. I'm taking pills now instead of the liquid medicine. I take two different kinds; one is for pain relief and the other is supposed to keep the JRA from getting worse. They have names so long I can't even pronounce them. I'm telling you this in the P.S. even though it is the most important news because I didn't want to write it at all. It's too awful.

February 27

Dear Mrs. Kaplan,

Today was the first day to sign up for the Fun Run. Gabby, Keelie, and I signed up during morning recess.

Each sponsor sheet has room for fifteen sponsors. I probably won't get that many because it is hard for me to ask people to give me money, even for a good cause like new playground equipment. I don't know what I'll be when I grow up, but I know I won't be a salesperson.

I plan to sponsor myself. It's a four-mile run, so if I sponsor myself for fifty cents a mile, that would use up one week's allowance. Maybe I'll sponsor myself twice, for twenty-five cents a mile each time, and use a fake name for one of them. That way I can fill in two lines instead of one on the sponsor sheet.

Here is Mrs. Lumbard's pen-pal question for this week: Did you have a favorite pet when you were a child?

Itty Bitty Kitty has a new place to sleep during the day. She crawls up on my bed underneath the bed-spread. I can tell when she's there because there's a lump under the spread. She has a nice soft cat bed, but she never sleeps there.

Today Mrs. Lumbard told my class that I have JRA. I knew she was going to do it.

I now get stiff if I sit in one place for more than fifteen minutes, so every fifteen minutes I have to get up and walk around the room. Mrs. Lumbard said it is fine for me to do that, but she had to tell the other kids why she let me do it and nobody else.

I'm glad now that I told Sarah and Gabby the truth a long time ago. It would have been a shock today if they still thought I had a brain tumor.

I decided to memorize the encyclopedia headings, too. I knew many of them already, from listening to Frankie repeat them all the time, so it wasn't too hard to learn the rest.

He skips the headings that have no information, only a referral to a different heading. Boy, am I glad about that. It would take twice as long if we included those and we wouldn't learn anything new. For example, after *Dash* it says, "See *Punctuation*," so we didn't include *Dash*.

I worked on my memorizing while Frankie was at soccer practice and Cub Scouts. Also, instead of covering my ears and leaving the room when he says them, I stick around and listen.

This morning at breakfast I decided to surprise him. I said, "If you start at the beginning, how far can you get?"

Frankie began saying the headings, and I said them

with him. He made it all the way to *Lakewood, Lakewood, Lakewood.* (That's right, there are three Lakewood headings. They are all cities: one in California, one in Colorado, and one in Ohio.) I only had to drop out a few times, and I always picked it up again.

The farther we got, the louder we talked. We beat our fists on the table every time we said a word.

Frankie got so excited that he tipped over his orange juice.

Dad said, "What did I do to deserve such exceptional children?"

I think it was a compliment.

Bye for now,
Julie

March 4

Dear Mrs. Kaplan,

Thank you for sending three dollars to sponsor me in the Fun Run. You are the only sponsor who volunteered. I had to ask everyone else.

It wasn't too hard, though. My grandparents, Papa and Nana, always say yes when I have to sell something for school. So do Mom and Dad. Most of my neighbors said yes, too, except for Mr. Limbet, who was already sponsoring his niece.

Frankie and I walked around the neighborhood together and took turns asking. That way people did not have to sponsor both of us.

Your letter surprised the whole class. The other fifth-grade pen pals all had dogs or cats for pets, plus one horse. You are the only one who had a pig. None of us knew that pigs are as intelligent as dogs.

It must have been fun to train your pig to do tricks. I tried to teach Itty Bitty Kitty to jump over a stick, but she won't do it. The only trick she knows is to run to the kitchen when she hears the can opener.

I went to the clinic yesterday to see Dr. McLean

(waiting time: twenty-two minutes; no current magazines) because the new pills gave me a rash.

So now I get a different kind of pill that is bigger and harder to swallow. Yuck. I told Mom I would be able to choke them down if I could follow them with a Reese's Peanut Butter Cup each time. She gave me her look that means *You are being absurd, and you know it.*

Dr. McLean says each case is different and it may take awhile to find the medication that's right for me.

Dad says, "Hang in there."

I say, "Phooey."

Your disgusted JRA pen pal,

Julie

P.S. Here is the most ridiculous thing I ever heard: There is a heading in the encyclopedia for *Encyclopedia!* Then there is a whole paragraph explaining that an encyclopedia is a reference work, and it tells how to use it to find information.

So if anyone does not know what an encyclopedia is, he can go to the encyclopedia and look it up!

March 10

Dear Mrs. Kaplan,

Something terrible is happening. I am not going to tell anyone but you.

The new medicine is not working. The old medicine for pain has quit working, too. My legs are worse and I ache all the time. It's hard to go up steps (it's a good thing my bedroom is downstairs now), and if I walk just a few blocks, my legs hurt so much I can hardly move. I have a terrible time getting on the school bus. I'm pretty sure I'm having another flare, and I never got over the last one.

I get tired so quickly now. I've quit going out to recess because playing games wears me out. I go to the library instead.

I am not going to tell Mom and Dad, because I am sick of going to doctors and occupational therapists. If my parents knew how much trouble I'm having, I'd be back in Dr. McLean's waiting room reading last year's *Time* magazines, and next I'd be lying as still as a stone under the X-ray machine, and then who knows what else, and what good does it do? There's no cure for JRA and none of the medicine helps, so why take more tests?

I know I'm whining. I'm sorry. But it's so awful that I had to tell someone, and you're the only one who will understand.

My friends don't want to hear about it. I think it makes them nervous that *they* might get JRA even though they know it isn't contagious. Besides, as Sarah proved when she thought I had a brain tumor, I can't trust them to keep their mouths shut.

Unhappy beyond belief,
Julie

March 13

To Mrs. Kaplan the Double-Crosser,

You will notice I no longer address you as "dear." I would not be writing to you at all, except Mrs. Lumbard is requiring us to do a pen-pal letter before we can go to lunch today.

I thought you were my friend. Boy, was I wrong.

Here is how I know what you did.

When I got home from school last Thursday, Mom said, "We need to have a talk."

Right away I tried to think what Frankie and I had done that would get me in trouble. I couldn't think of anything except the day before we had eaten all of the Heath Bar Crunch ice cream while Mom was writing letters, but Mom's look was not her *You little pig, you ate all the ice cream* look, it was more serious.

She said your daughter had called. She told Mom that I am having a lot of stiffness and pain in my legs.

You knew I wasn't going to tell anyone but you. Especially not Mom and Dad. Why did you betray me?

You probably are not reading this letter because

Mrs. Lumbard won't mail it. She says she does not read the pen-pal letters that we write in class before she mails them, but I bet she does when no one is looking. I don't trust adults anymore.

Your former friend,

Julie

March 18

Dear, dear Mrs. Kaplan,

Can you ever forgive me?

I didn't know that while I was accusing you of being a traitor you were in the hospital, too sick to read your mail, and that is why your daughter opened my letter and called Mom.

I should have known you would not do such a thing. I'm sorry I suspected you, and I hope you are feeling better now.

Did the doctors order a bunch of tests on you? Did they X-ray your bones? Did they stick a needle in your arm and take out all your blood? I hope not.

I'm glad to know you are out of the hospital and back at Shady Villa. Even if you don't get enchiladas there, anything is better than being in the hospital.

I had to go back to Dr. McLean and have more tests, and I was right: I am having another flare. It's pretty bad this time. I may have to get a walker to help me walk. I don't want one. Dr. McLean says they come in different colors and have a basket on the front to carry stuff in, and a seat that folds down if I get tired. I still don't want one.

I am worried about the talent contest. My knuckles are swollen and my fingers don't work right. They actually feel hot. If I don't get a lot better, I'll never make it through "Boogie-Woogie Blues" and my only chance to earn a trophy for Adams School will be gone forever.

Dr. McLean gave me some grippers to put on my pencils to make them fatter and easier for me to hold. I'm using one to write this letter and it helps a lot. I'm not going to use it at school, though. The other kids would think I'm a baby who needs a big, fat kindergarten pencil. No, thanks.

I am worried about the Fun Run, too. What if I can't do it?

Dad says, "Think positive."

Mom says, "Quit fretting. You'll create a self-fulfilling prophecy."

I say, "JRA stands for Junky Rotten Affliction."

Your friend forever,
Julie

P.S. The only good news I have is that I took the *M* book of the encyclopedia to the doctor with me. While I sat in the waiting room, I memorized fourteen pages.

Dear Mrs. Kaplan,

The assembly on recycling was today. It was so much fun. I got to sit on the stage because I introduced Mr. Irving, the man I met at the Home and Garden Show. His talk was great. He showed slides of all the products that are made from old car tires.

At the end, as the kids left the gym, the teachers handed out pencils made from recycled jeans and old money. All the kids thought those were really cool.

When Mr. Irving finished talking, Mr. Randolph reminded everyone that my next litter pickup day is on Saturday. He said there will be free ice cream at the end of the pickup. That was news to me!

Mr. Randolph's brother owns an ice-cream store, and he said he wants to encourage kids not to litter. Aren't people nice?

Well, most people are. Something is really bugging me. Every day when I come to school, I find an empty root-beer can on the sidewalk by Adams Fountain. Every day I pick it up and put it in the recycle bin.

I would sure like to know who leaves a can there every day. Tomorrow Frankie and I are going to go to school early; Dad said he would drop us off on his way to work. We are going to hide in the library and peek out the window to see if we can catch the culprit.

We are out of postage stamps so I can't mail this.

The next day

Frankie and I got to school a whole half hour early, but the root-beer can was already there. Someone must leave it at night.

Since we didn't catch the root-beer-can maniac, we used the half hour before school started to practice saying the encyclopedia headings. We are already on the *N*'s.

Keelie lives only two blocks from school. She is going to go over there after dinner tonight to see if she can find out who the litterbug is.

Friday

Keelie played on the monkey bars and kept an eye on the fountain, but she did not see anyone drinking root beer. She stayed until it started to get dark. The fountain area was clean when she left, but the empty can was there this morning. This is a real mystery.

Tomorrow is the second official litter pickup day. Thirty-eight kids have signed up to help. The PTA has parents coming to supervise. With that much help we'll get the whole school yard finished, plus all the neighborhood. I hope it doesn't rain.

I also hope I can work the whole two hours. When my legs are real sore, it's hard for me to stand that long.

Saturday night

Wow! What a great day! Forty-two kids and seven parents came to the litter pickup. There is not a scrap of paper or a pull tab from a soda pop can within six blocks of Adams School. It looks like a brand-new school.

The garbage company brought us extra recycle containers and some gigantic plastic garbage bags, and we filled all of them.

Two of the parents started singing, "I've been working on the school yard, all the live long day," to the tune of "I've Been Working on the Railroad," and pretty soon we all were singing at the top of our lungs.

The only bad part was that my legs ached so much and I got so tired that I had to quit partway through and sit by the fountain and watch.

A third grader saw me sitting there when everyone else was working and said, "What are you, the boss?"

Sarah heard him. She said, "Julie has a terrible disease that makes her legs hurt, and sometimes she can't even walk."

The third grader's eyes got really big and he said, "Oh. Sorry."

I'm glad Sarah was there, but I hate it when things like that happen. I'd rather just pick up the trash like everyone else.

I got your letter today. I may try what you said and give pencil grippers to my best friends. The grippers are fun to use, and I would like to use mine at school because it makes it a lot easier for me to write.

Monday

The root-beer-can maniac struck again! There was not a single bit of trash on the school yard this morning except another stupid root-beer can. It was actually floating in Adams Fountain!

If I ever get my hands on who is doing this, he or she will be sorry. The next time I see one of those carpenter ants, I will not flush it down the toilet, I will bring it to school and leave it in the dirt by Adams Fountain. Maybe it will crawl up the pants of the root-beer-can maniac.

You were right about the pencil grippers. I gave one to Sarah, one to Gabby, and one to Keelie, and they like them. We all used them at school today, and now the other kids are begging me to get pencil grippers for them. Frankie was the star of his class because he was the only third grader who had a pencil gripper.

Sarah, Gabby, Keelie, and I are making posters about the Fun Run. They'll hang in the cafeteria and in the gym.

We finally have stamps. I'm going to mail this today or my news will be so old it won't be news any more.

Your pen pal,

Julie

NOTICE TO MRS. KAPLAN'S DAUGHTER,
SUSAN BERG
THIS LETTER IS PRIVATE. DO NOT READ.
I REPEAT: *DO NOT READ!!*

March 29

Dear Mrs. Kaplan,

I hope your daughter won't be mad if she sees that, but it bothers me when someone else reads my private words to you. I'm sure Susan is a very nice person and I know she only wanted to help me when she called Mom, but still, snooping is snooping, if you ask me.

I have another problem and I need some advice. I hope you don't mind listening to my troubles. My friends are no help.

I asked Gabby if she has any problems, and she said, "Yes. My bike is too small and my parents won't buy me a bigger one."

All I said was "Oh," but I wanted to say, "You call that a problem? Try not being able to ride a bike at all!"

The problem is the Fun Run that Sarah is in charge of. This is part of a statewide program and there is a terrific prize for any school where one hundred percent of the students finish the race.

Sarah made a huge chart shaped like a thermometer.

At the bottom is zero, and at the top it says THREE HUNDRED TWELVE. That's how many kids go to Adams School.

Every day Sarah goes to the school office and collects the Fun Run sign-up sheets that have been turned in. She counts them and then she uses a bright red marker and colors in the thermometer up to the right number. So far two hundred and four kids have signed up, so the thermometer is colored red two-thirds of the way up.

Today on the morning announcements, Sarah got to talk over the public address system. She said if every Adams student finishes the run, we not only get the sponsor's money for new playground equipment, we'll get a new book for the school library for every single kid. That means three hundred and twelve new books!

During the first recess after her announcement, dozens of kids went to the office to get sign-up sheets to take home.

Here is the problem: I'm afraid I won't be able to finish the race. My legs are getting worse and worse, and I get so tired. When Mom called Dr. McLean, he said I should get a walker now so I'll have it if I need it.

I don't want to get a walker now. I don't want to have a walker at all. There is no way I would be able to walk four miles even with a walker.

What if I'm the only kid in Adams School who

doesn't finish the Fun Run? After all of Sarah's hard work, the school would lose out on three hundred and twelve new library books just because of me. Nobody would ever talk to me again.

Your worried friend,
Julie

April 2

Dear Mrs. Kaplan,

I'm glad to know you are feeling better and that Susan has gone back to her family in Ohio.

I took your advice and asked Sarah for a copy of the Fun Run rules. You were right. The rules say that one hundred percent participation means every student "unless he or she has a written excuse from a parent stating there was a family emergency, or a medical excuse signed by a physician."

I go to see Dr. McLean tomorrow. I'm going to ask him to write me a medical excuse. That way I won't let anybody down if I can't do the race.

Frankie knows I have been worrying about the Fun Run. He suggested that we put our sponsors together and enter the race as one person. He said I could go as far as I could and then he would finish.

It's nice of Frankie to offer to do that because he is a fast runner and will do good by himself. I told him I don't want to race together; I want to do it on my own or not at all.

I have a new plan to catch the root-beer can maniac. During every recess I sit near the soda pop machine and watch to see who buys root beer. I never buy soda pop because Mom says it's too expensive and it will make my teeth fall out, but lots of kids do buy it. I figure if I know which ones drink root beer, I will have a list of suspects.

So far there are six names on my list, including Evelyn Gilmore and Bo-Bob Jersey. (John Jersey bought Pepsi; maybe they are not identical twins.) Mr. Randolph bought root beer, too, but he wouldn't leave his can by Adams Fountain. I don't think Evelyn Gilmore would, either. (Remember her "Do What's Right" bracelet?) That leaves Bo-Bob and four others. I am keeping an eye on them.

Frankie and I are now on the *P*'s in the encyclopedia. When Frankie was reciting the headings of the encyclopedia alone, it drove me crazy to hear him, but now that I am learning them, too, I like to hear him practice. Isn't that odd?

Dad says, "If you can't beat 'em, join 'em." Maybe he's right.

The hardest part of memorizing the encyclopedia headings is that every time I look to see what comes next, I get interested in what it says about each topic, and I end up reading a couple of pages. I've learned a lot of fascinating information that way (did you know that hummingbirds can fly backward?), but it also slows me down in learning the headings.

After I go to bed at night, I start with *A* and see how far I can get before I fall asleep. Last night I dozed off somewhere between *Lily of the Valley* and *Lima Bean*.

Yours 'til Niagara Falls,

Julie

Dear Mrs. Kaplan,

I got checked by Dr. McLean again yesterday. I had something called an MRI, which is sort of like an X-ray.

My hands are a lot better since I started this medicine, but my legs just keep getting worse.

Dad says, "Half a loaf is better than none."

I fail to see what bread has to do with it.

Now I get two kinds of medicine every six hours. I guess I can stand to go to the nurse's office to take yucky pills every day during recess if it keeps my fingers flexible, because that means Gabby and I have a chance to win the talent contest.

The contest is next Tuesday and we are practicing like crazy. We plan to wear matching outfits. The judges don't give points for appearance, but it can't hurt to look good.

I asked Dr. McLean to write me an excuse for the Fun Run. He did, but he told me not to turn it in until the day of the race. He said my legs might get better and I would want to run. He said sometimes it takes several weeks for a new medicine to work. I hope he's right.

If my legs hurt too much for me to run, I will give all of my sponsors to Frankie so they don't go to waste. I hope that is okay with you.

I know I told you Frankie is sneaky and devious, but that is only when he's thinking up mischief. Since he's had his mind on our encyclopedia project, we have not been in trouble hardly at all. It's hard to think up pranks when your brain is racing from *Pineapple* to *Ping-Pong* to *Pink.*

Dr. McLean had a new idea for me. He suggested that I get a wheelchair to use for part of the Fun Run. He said I could borrow one from the clinic. He said other JRA patients have participated in running events by using a wheelchair.

I really don't want to use a wheelchair, but if I had to, at least I would be doing the whole race by myself. When I got home, I called Sarah and told her Dr. McLean's idea.

She said, "Do it! I've been afraid that you will hurt yourself by trying to run. If you use a wheelchair, I won't have to worry about you."

Isn't that something? All the time I've been worried about letting Sarah down, she's been worrying that I'll overdo it.

Dad says, "A true friend always wants what's best for you." I think Sarah is a true friend.

Now here is the surprise news of the century: Two days after I started writing down the names of everyone who buys root beer at school, the maniac quit leaving his cans by the fountain! I've been keeping my list for a week now, and there has not been a single root-beer can littering the school since last Wednesday.

Isn't that incredible? Maybe I have solved the problem without solving the mystery. The only trouble is, I use up all my recess sitting around looking at the soda pop machine. It gets pretty boring.

Wish Gabby and me luck next Tuesday,
Julie

P.S. While I was in the *P*'s, I learned that there are twenty-five varieties of popcorn. That made me so hungry that I quit memorizing and fixed a snack.

April 5

Dear Mrs. Kaplan,

I know I just wrote to you yesterday, but you will not believe what happened. I had to go see Dr. McLean again today, even though I was just there yesterday, because I stepped on Itty Bitty Kitty's catnip mouse and lost my balance, and fell down and hurt my ankle.

Mom was afraid I had broken something. I was afraid I would have to stay in the hospital.

Dr. McLean X-rayed my ankle, and he said I sprained it and tore the ligaments. I have to use crutches for a month. This means I'll be on crutches for the talent contest and also for the Fun Run. Even without JRA I don't think I could go four miles on crutches.

My ankle hurts a lot. It's a different kind of hurt than JRA. JRA is a deep ache; this is a sharp pain. I am sitting on my bed with my foot propped up on two pillows and an ice pack on my ankle.

Mom asked if she could bring me anything, and I said, "Yes, a hot-fudge sundae," but she said that isn't what she meant. I had her bring me Itty Bitty Kitty instead, and she is now purring next to me, unaware that her catnip mouse caused all this grief.

Your sprained and torn friend,

Julie

April 6

Dear Mrs. Kaplan,

Well, here I am in time-out again and I didn't do anything. How unfair can parents be?

This is what happened: My ankle quit throbbing last night, so I decided to try out my crutches. It took me awhile to get used to them. I clunked into things such as doorways a lot because I forgot that the crutches are wider than I am, but after a while I was walking really well.

My legs don't hurt so much when I use the crutches. My armpits are sore, though.

Frankie kept begging and begging for a turn to use the crutches. I wouldn't let him try them yesterday because I had to learn how myself and they are my crutches. He started asking again after school today, and by then I was tired anyway, so I told him he could use them for a while.

The crutches were too tall for Frankie, so he turned them upside down. He held on to the pointed ends and put his feet on the handholds. The part that was supposed to go under his arms went on the ground.

"Look!" he said. "I'm taller than you are!"

He actually kept his balance and lurched all around the yard using my crutches like stilts.

By the time Dad saw him and made him stop, the armrests were all muddy and grass-stained.

That's when Frankie and I got sent to time-out. The crutches are rented for a month, but if we take them back all stained, we may have to buy them.

I pointed out that I had done nothing except watch, and Dad said, "That makes you an accomplice."

Wouldn't you think there would be some sympathy for a JRA girl who has a sprained ankle, torn ligaments, sore armpits, dirty crutches, and a wacky little brother? Not around here.

I thought I would feel like a freak using crutches at school today, but it was fun. Sarah and Gabby offered to carry my backpack for me because it's hard to get it on and off while I'm holding my crutches.

Everyone else made a big fuss over me, which seems odd because nobody makes a fuss over my having JRA and that is way worse than a sprained ankle.

Maybe it wouldn't be so bad to get a walker.

Tomorrow is the talent show. Keep your fingers crossed.

Your friend,
Julie

April 8

Dear Mrs. Kaplan,

The talent contest turned out much different than I expected! Here is what happened: Gabby and I practiced until we knew our duet by heart. I think we could have played "Boogie-Woogie Blues" backward if we had wanted to.

We wore white blouses and dark skirts, and we both braided our hair and put red ribbons on the braids. I don't mean to brag, but we looked really good.

We were ready!

Then something terrible happened. On the night of the talent show, Gabby got the flu. We worried for weeks that my fingers would be too stiff to play well, and it turned out Gabby was the one who couldn't do it.

She started feeling sick soon after we got to the school that night.

There was pizza backstage for all the contestants. At first I thought Gabby didn't feel well because she had eaten too much pizza, but she said she didn't have any.

Her mom said Gabby had stage fright, which meant she was nervous about our duet.

The talent show was supposed to start at seven o'clock; we were to be the first act after the intermission.

At one minute before seven Gabby threw up.

Gabby's mom took her to the nurse's office and made her lie down, and she took Gabby's temperature and it was one hundred and two. So her mom came and told me that Gabby could not play "Boogie-Woogie Blues" with me in the talent show.

There I stood, ready to go out onstage in my red hair ribbons, and half of my act was in the nurse's office throwing up. I almost cried.

I probably would have except Sarah, who was backstage waiting to do her tap-dance routine, said, "Why don't you do your encyclopedia trick with your brother?"

I never thought it took talent to memorize the headings of the encyclopedia, but at that point I was desperate. During the intermission I found Mom, Dad, and Frankie in the audience and told them about Gabby and asked Frankie if he wanted to be the substitute act. He did.

We went backstage and told Mr. Randolph. We almost didn't make it in time because the crutches really slow me down.

When intermission ended, Mr. Randolph announced, "There is one change in the program. The next act will be Julie and Frankie Welsh, who will recite the headings of the encyclopedia."

Frankie and I walked out to the microphone. Fortunately, Mom and Dad had made him take a shower and wear clean clothes. For once, he didn't have a hole in the knee of his jeans.

We looked at each other for a second. I nodded and together we launched into *"Aardvark, Aardwolf, Aaron."*

We had done it so many times that those headings just rolled off our tongues. By the time we got to the *B*'s we were talking so fast we barely paused between headings, and when we got to the *C*'s, the audience started to clap. They clapped and clapped and I wondered how they could even hear us, but Frankie and I just kept going until in the middle of the *G*'s, Mr. Randolph held up his hand and said, "Your time is up."

Someone in the auditorium yelled out, "Let them finish!"

Mr. Randolph said, "In fairness to the other contestants, I have to enforce the time limit, but I have no doubt that Julie and Frankie can say the headings all the way through the *Z*'s."

Actually we can only go to the *T*'s, but I didn't say that.

Everyone clapped some more.

When the contest was over, it took the judges about ten minutes to add up all the points. Then Mr. Randolph went onstage and announced the winners.

Third place went to a girl in fourth grade who had played "Flight of the Bumblebee" on the piano. She was really good; her piece made the "Boogie-Woogie Blues" duet sound as simple as "Chopsticks." Gabby and I would never have won.

Sarah got second place for her tap-dance routine.

Then Mr. Randolph said, "First place goes to Julie and Frankie Welsh, for memorizing the headings of the encyclopedia. They will represent Adams School in the district talent competition."

The district contest is not for six weeks. We plan to know the whole encyclopedia by then, in case the time limit is longer. If we win the district contest, Adams School gets the trophy!

Your first-place friend,
Julie

P.S. Oops. I did it again. I blabbed on and on about me when I'm supposed to ask about you. Here is this week's question: If you could go back to any place you ever went, where would you go?

April 11

Dear Mrs. Kaplan,

You really surprised me this time. I thought your favorite place would be Alaska or the Panama Canal or that part of Africa where you went on safari and photographed the elephants.

I was shocked when you said if you could take a trip anywhere in the world you would go back to a white frame house in Kansas City where you lived when Susan was small.

Dad says, "To each his own," but I thought your own would be someplace more exotic.

If I could go anywhere in the world, I would go to Disney World. Mom and Dad say it costs too much. They say that about a lot of things.

I wonder if we would be able to afford Disney World if I didn't have JRA. We have health insurance through Dad's company, but we still have to pay for part of the medicine and some of the doctor bills.

We had to rent my crutches, too, and if I have to get a walker, we'll need to buy that.

I just thought of something. I complain that it isn't fair that I have to go to bed before Frankie does, because I have JRA. But if I didn't have JRA maybe we could go to Disney World, so it really isn't fair to Frankie, either. He misses out on Disney World because of my Junky Rotten Affliction.

I got invited to a sleep-over party at Keelie's house. I almost said I couldn't come because I was worried about having to take a bath the next morning. I really want to go, so Mom called Keelie's mom and explained how I have to soak in a warm bath for twenty minutes as soon as I get up every day, to help my joints loosen up, and Keelie's mom said that would be no problem. Some of the things I worry about turn out not to be any trouble, after all.

Mom went to the clinic today and borrowed the wheelchair, so if I need to use it to finish the Fun Run on Saturday, I can.

All 4 now,

Julie

P.S. I have stopped watching the soda pop machine at recess. I missed out on too much fun with my friends. Three days after I quit, there was a root-beer can by the fountain, and I've found one there every day since. It's disgusting, but I'd rather pick up the maniac's trash every morning than miss recess.

It takes only five seconds to toss that root-beer can in the recycle bin; recess lasts twenty minutes, twice a day.

Dad always says, "Use your time wisely." So I am.

April 14

Dear Mrs. Kaplan,

The wheelchair idea is not going to work for the Fun Run. I practiced wheeling around in it today, and my arms got really sore and tired. I hurt more after using the wheelchair than I do when I walk with the crutches.

If I had been using a wheelchair for a while, it would be different.

Dad said he is willing to rent an electric wheelchair for one day, but I said that would be like cheating.

The Fun Run is tomorrow. Do you suppose a miraculous cure for JRA will be discovered during the night?

Your worried friend,

Julie

April 16

Dear Mrs. Kaplan,

Yesterday was the Fun Run. Here is what happened:

All the runners were supposed to be checked in at the school by eight o'clock. The race started at eight-thirty.

I set my alarm for six-thirty. I knew as soon as I woke up that I was in trouble. Some days are better for me than others and I could tell that it was not going to be one of the good days.

I soaked longer than usual in the tub, got dressed, and ate some Wheaties® (Breakfast of Champions®), but my knee and hip joints already hurt just from the little effort of moving around my bedroom and kitchen.

My ankle doesn't bother me much anymore, but the crutches are awkward and slow me down. (I'm plenty slow without them.)

By the time Frankie came into the kitchen, I had made up my mind.

"I'm not going to do the race," I told him. "I'll go to cheer for you and my friends, but I'm going to turn in my excuse from Dr. McLean."

For once in his life Frankie was quiet. He thought

about it for a minute, and then he said, "You have to try. If you don't, you'll always wish you had."

It was my turn to be quiet.

Finally I said, "Sarah will understand."

"Yes, she will," Frankie said. "If you don't do the race, everyone will understand. But if you give it your best shot, whether you finish or not, all your friends will be proud of you for trying."

"It's easy for you to say," I said. "Your legs don't ache."

"I know," Frankie said. To my astonishment, he blinked back tears. "I hate it that you hurt so much. It isn't fair."

"What if I start the race and can't finish it?" I said. "Then it's too late to turn in my excuse from Dr. McLean and the school will lose out on all those free books."

"No way," Frankie said. "The Fun Run sponsors would honor your excuse. If they didn't, every kid in Adams School would protest."

"I don't want to start and then have to drop out."

"What about the wheelchair?"

"My arm muscles are even more sore today than they were last night. If I was going to do the race in a wheelchair, I should have started practicing a couple of weeks ago."

"I'll push you in the wheelchair."

I shook my head. "If I do the race, I have to do it myself."

I thought about what he had said, about giving it my best shot. I thought about how Sarah had suggested that Frankie and I do our encyclopedia trick so I could still be in the talent contest, even though she was a contestant herself and ended up losing to us.

I thought about all the times Sarah and Gabby and Keelie had walked slowly so I could keep up with them and how Gabby never complained when I didn't want to practice our duet and how all of my friends faithfully helped with litter pickup.

"You won't let your friends down if you try and can't finish," Frankie said. "You'll only let them down if you don't try."

I knew he was right. I had to try. I wanted my friends to feel proud of me. I wanted to feel proud of myself.

"Let's go," I said.

When we got to the school, Frankie jumped out of the car and headed for the check-in station. As I got out, Mom said, "You can still change your mind, Julie. No one will think less of you if you use the letter Dr. McLean wrote for you."

"I want to try," I said.

Mom nodded. "I admire you for that," she said, "but don't push yourself. If it hurts too much or you get too tired, stop. We can use the wheelchair to get you back to the car."

As I checked in, Keelie and Gabby came over. "Are

you going to try to do the race on your crutches?" Keelie asked.

"Yes."

They didn't seem as glad as I had expected.

"We thought you would use the excuse from your doctor," Gabby said.

"Sarah was positive you would do the race," Keelie said, "but we thought it would be too hard."

"Where is Sarah?" I asked.

"Running around like a hyperactive two-year-old," Keelie said. "She feels responsible for everything today."

Gabby and Keelie kept glancing at each other as if they knew a secret and weren't sure whether to tell me.

Finally Gabby said, "We need to ask you something, but we're afraid we'll hurt your feelings."

"What is it?" I asked.

"Promise you won't get mad?" Keelie said.

"I promise."

"When the run starts," Gabby said, "would you mind if we keep up with the rest of the fifth grade? We want to see how many fifth graders can finish before the rest of the school, and we know you won't be able to go that fast, with your crutches."

"I don't mind," I said. "I want you to run with the other fifth graders."

I was lying. I did mind. I minded a lot—not that they wanted to run with the other fifth graders; I could understand that. I minded that I couldn't run with them, too.

Just then Mr. Randolph yelled, "Kindergartners at the starting line! First grade behind them! Get in your places, everyone."

Parents and teachers began making sure all of the kids were lined up with the proper grade.

Although the fifth grade started last, nobody complained. We all agreed that letting the younger kids have a head start was the only fair way.

What about kids with JRA? I thought as everyone jostled into position. Maybe they should get a head start, too. Like about two days.

As head of the Fun Run, Sarah got to ring a big brass bell when it was time for each grade to begin. *Ding! Ding!* went the bell. "Go, Kindergarten!" Sarah yelled.

A minute later the bell bonged again, and Sarah hollered, "Go, First Grade!" Then it was "Go, Second Grade!"

When she yelled "Go, Third Grade!" I saw Frankie take off. Frankie's a good runner, and he was already passing some of the second-grade kids before he even got to the corner.

It took only a couple of minutes more for Sarah to shout, "Go, Fifth Grade!" As the fifth graders rushed across the starting line, Sarah handed the bell to Mr. Randolph and rushed to join Gabby and Keelie.

I was the last to start. I was afraid if I started in the middle of the group someone would trip on one of my crutches and either I would go down or the person who tripped would. Since I had no chance of winning the race anyway, I decided to be safe and take off after everyone else had left.

The first few blocks were actually fun. Lots of relatives and friends of the runners stood on the curbs and sidewalks to cheer as the runners went past. When they saw that I was doing the race on crutches, they cheered for me, too.

By the time I had gone four blocks, the onlookers had left. They thought all of the runners had already gone by. All of them had, except me.

After about fifteen minutes my legs really started to hurt. To distract myself from the pain, I began thinking of the titles of my favorite books and how great it would be if our library got extra copies of them.

The PTA had parents stationed along the race course, at the one-mile mark, the two-mile mark, and the three-mile mark. The parents had bandages in case anyone got a blister, and paper cups full of cold water for those who wanted a drink. There were even a couple of folding chairs.

Mom was working at the first station, which was one-fourth of the way through the race.

"Are you sure you should continue?" she asked.

"Yes," I panted.

I sat on one of the chairs, trying to catch my breath. I felt as if I had already walked twenty miles instead of only one.

She gave me her *I don't agree, but I'll let you have your way for now* look. When I reached for a cup of water, she said, "Take these," and gave me two of the pills I take for pain.

I must have looked surprised because she added, "It's okay. I checked with Dr. McLean when I picked up the wheelchair."

I swallowed the pills gratefully, hoping they would work quickly. Maybe with extra pills to mask the pain I would be able to finish.

I started back along the race course. It wasn't just my legs that hurt; my hands were sore from gripping the crossbar on the crutches, and my upper arms still ached from pushing the wheelchair the day before.

That morning I had been ready to use JRA as an excuse not to run. As I started the second mile, I wondered if I had been foolish to let Frankie talk me into trying the race.

The more I hurt, the more convinced I was that it was all Frankie's fault. Why had I listened to him? What did he know about having JRA except he got to stay up later than I did?

Sweat trickled down the back of my neck.

I didn't know if the extra pain pills had helped or not. I hurt just as much as before I took them, but maybe I would hurt even more if I had not taken them.

Pain wasn't my only problem. The fatigue was even worse. All I wanted to do was lie down and rest.

I plodded on, determined not to quit until I at least reached the second water-break station, which was halfway through the course. Halfway wouldn't be too bad. Two whole miles on crutches was nothing to sneeze at.

I had to look down most of the time because I was afraid I would trip on something, but I glanced up frequently in order to set small goals for myself.

I will keep going until I pass that telephone pole, I thought, and then when I reached the telephone pole, I looked up and set a new goal: *I will not stop until after I pass that big maple tree.*

I knew I was tricking myself, but it didn't matter. It felt good to achieve those small goals, especially when I feared that I would not be able to achieve the day's real goal: finishing the race.

I tried to imagine myself crossing the finish line— and couldn't do it. It was too far, and I was too tired, and I hurt too much.

Just make it to the second break station, I thought. *Just make it halfway through the race before you quit.*

Far ahead I heard cheering and music playing, and I knew that the other runners had finished. I felt utterly alone. I wasn't even halfway through, and the rest of the kids were already done.

Did anyone care that I was struggling down the street by myself? Would anyone even notice whether I finished the race or not?

I could sit down right now, I thought, and wait for Mom and Dad to come by in the car and pick me up, and Adams School would probably still get the free library books.

But what if someone *did* notice? What if a representative from the company who had made the free-book offer was sitting at the finish line counting heads? What if he got to three hundred and eleven and then said, "Too bad, Adams School. You missed it by one."

Everyone would know who it was that didn't finish. The whole school would be mad at me.

Tears dripped off my chin and splashed onto my T-shirt. I didn't bother to wipe them away. I knew I wasn't crying about the library books. Deep down, I knew Adams School would get the books even if I didn't finish the race. I cried because I was tired—tired of not being able to keep up, tired of being different, tired of having JRA.

After what seemed an eternity, I saw the sign ahead for the second station—but nobody was there! I learned later that the parents who had given out drinks of water to the other three hundred and eleven runners had left to congregate at the finish line and watch the end of the race.

I walked to the table anyway, leaned my crutches against it, and sat on a folding chair. I had made it halfway.

As soon as I sat down, I felt better. Maybe, I thought, if I rest a little while, I can walk some more. I closed my eyes.

"How are you doing?" Frankie's voice startled me; I had not heard him coming.

"I don't think I can make it."

"Sure you can. I'll help you."

"What are you going to do, carry me?"

"No. But I did bring the wheelchair. Mom's helping some kid who fell, so she had me bring it."

"Did you already finish the race?" I asked.

"No. I came back to find you. It will be so cool to have you walk across that finish line that I want to see you do it."

When he said that, I imagined it happening. I saw myself finishing the race, and that mental image made me want to do it more than I had ever wanted anything in my life.

I stood up. I winced when I put my crutches under my arms.

"What's the matter?" Frankie asked.

"I'm sore from leaning on the crutches so much."

"That's the pits," Frankie said. He grinned, waiting for me to acknowledge his joke.

I groaned.

"I'll push the wheelchair," Frankie said. "If you want it, it's here."

"Thanks," I said. He had given up his chance to win the race in order to come back and walk with me, but I was too weary to say anything more than "Thanks."

"Let's say the encyclopedia headings while we walk," Frankie suggested. "That will keep your mind off your aches."

"You'll have to start at the beginning. I can't pick it up in the middle."

"Aardvark," Frankie said. *"Aardwolf. Aaron."*

I joined in. *"Abacus. Abalone. Abandonment."*

Frankie was right; thinking about the headings of the encyclopedia did help. By the time we got to *Alphabet,* I was concentrating so much that I hardly noticed the pain.

We had just said *"Loon"* when I saw the third and last water-break station ahead.

Mom was there. She handed me a cup of water. "You need to sit," she said.

I sank onto a chair.

"She's doing great," Frankie said. "She's going to finish the race."

"Your legs hurt," Mom said. It was not a question, but I nodded, yes.

"And your arms?"

I nodded again.

"Pain is Nature's way of telling you that you need to stop what you are doing and rest," Mom said. "Listen to your body."

I knew she was right. I knew the last mile would be even harder on my body than the first three miles had been. *If* I could even make it one more mile.

"If you must continue, use the wheelchair," Mom said.

"I can't. My arms are too sore and tired to push it."

Frankie said, "I offered to push her."

"I want to try to finish by myself," I said.

I expected Mom to argue, but she didn't. She seemed to understand that this was not a day to listen to my body; this was a day to listen to my heart. I desperately wanted to finish that fourth mile.

Just then I saw a group of kids running toward us. I knew they were kids who had been in the race, because they each had a number pinned to their shirts.

When they got closer, I saw that Sarah, Gabby, and Keelie were in front, followed by what seemed like half the fifth grade. Mixed in with my classmates were some of Frankie's third-grade pals.

My friends rushed up to me. "We were eating our ice cream and you weren't there and we realized you probably had not finished," Gabby said.

"Not yet," I said, "but I'm going to."

I stood up.

"Your legs don't hurt too much?" Sarah said.

"They hurt plenty," Frankie said. "So do her arms

and hands. So does her back. But she's going to finish the race."

"Would it help if you leaned on us instead of using the crutches?" Gabby said. She stood close beside me and slid her arm around my waist. I put my arm around her shoulder.

Sarah hurried to get on my other side. She put her arm around my waist, too, and I laid mine around her shoulder.

"I'll take the crutches," Frankie said, "in case you need them." He laid them in the wheelchair.

"Ready?" Gabby said.

I took a deep breath. "Yes."

We started to walk, with Gabby and Sarah supporting me as I leaned on them. The other kids surrounded us. One group led the way, some walked beside us, and the rest trailed behind. All of them walked only as fast as I could walk.

I still hurt, and I was still tired, but it helped my arms to be rid of the crutches. And it felt great to know that my friends wanted to help me.

"You are the bravest girl I know," Sarah said.

"Who won the race?" I asked.

"John and Bo-Bob Jersey tied for first," Gabby said.

Keelie, who was walking beside Sarah, said, "The fifth graders beat all the other classes."

"I wish you could have been with us," Gabby said.

Before I could reply, the most amazing thing happened. The kids who were walking behind us began to chant my name. "Ju-lie. Ju-lie."

The rest of the kids quickly joined in. I was surrounded by "Ju-lie, Ju-lie."

Other kids who had finished the race heard the chorus and came to see what the commotion was. When they saw me struggling along, with Sarah and Gabby helping me, they joined the parade. The sound got louder and louder.

Soon the parents and other onlookers who had watched the race formed lines on each side of the street. As the kids chanting "Ju-lie, Ju-lie" approached, the spectators cheered. They clapped and whistled and yelled out encouragement as we passed.

"Way to go, Julie!"

"We're proud of you, Julie!"

I recognized one voice that rang out over the others. It was Dad. He yelled, "The real winner is the girl who's finishing last!"

The pain and fatigue did not go away, but they no longer mattered. My body felt weightless, buoyed by the friendship of my classmates. As I walked, a great sea of students surged forward with me, chanting, "Ju-lie. Ju-lie."

Frankie walked backward ahead of me, pulling the wheelchair with the crutches on the seat. A huge grin lit up his face. For once, I was glad I had done what my brother wanted.

When we were a block from the end, the group in

front of me split and moved to the sides to let me pass between them.

Ahead I saw the big white banner that said FINISH LINE. It was strung between two light poles, high above the street.

When I saw that banner, my arms and the back of my neck prickled with excitement. I was going to make it! Adams School would get all the new library books because runner number three hundred and twelve was going to finish the race.

I felt Sarah's hand and Gabby's hand tighten around my waist. I knew they were excited, too.

The voices shouting "JU-LIE! JU-LIE!" grew louder and louder until I felt the noise would lift me from my feet and I would fly up and over the FINISH LINE banner like a kite.

When we were inches away, Sarah and Gabby spontaneously let go of me.

Frankie handed me the crutches.

I walked across the finish line alone.

As cheers exploded all around me, Frankie said, "I knew you could do it."

He took the crutches and I sat in the wheelchair.

It had taken me almost three hours. Every inch of my body hurt, but I felt great!

It's better to finish last than not to try at all.

Your exhilarated pen pal,

Julie

P.S. When we got home from the Fun Run, Stupid But Essential told us to call Dr. McLean. I was uneasy because it was the first time the doctor had ever called us. It turned out he just wanted to know how I got along in the Fun Run.

When Mom told him what had happened, Dr. McLean said he would donate one hundred dollars to the playground fund in my honor! He also said I should stay in bed today, which was fine with me.

April 17

Dear Julie,

Thank you for all the letters you have written to my mother. She loves hearing from you, and your letters give her something special to look forward to.

This letter is from me instead of from her because she is too ill to write. She has cancer of the liver and her doctor says she will not live much longer.

Mother tells me not to feel sad, because she's had a long and happy life. Of course I am sad anyway. I know you will be sad, too, but I wanted you to know why you will not get any more pen-pal letters from her.

Best regards,

Susan Kaplan Berg

April 25

Dear Julie,

Your flowers arrived the day before my mother died. She was so pleased. Thank you for sending them.

She wasn't strong enough to dictate a letter, but she said to tell you to never give up.

Best regards,

Susan Berg

April 28

Dear Susan Berg,

I will always remember Mrs. Kaplan. She was the best pen pal in the fifth-grade project.

When I read your letter, I held Itty Bitty Kitty and cried so much her fur got soaked.

The saddest kid in the whole world,

Julie Welsh

May 10

Dear Julie,

When I emptied out Mother's dresser drawer, I found the letters you wrote to her. She had saved them all. I couldn't bear to throw them away when they had meant so much to her, so I am mailing them back to you, along with a copy of my mother's obituary from the newspaper.

Best regards,

Susan Berg

Dear Susan Berg,

Thank you for returning my letters. Mom put them in my save box, where we keep special things that I want to save forever.

I don't understand the obituary you sent. It says your mother was a homemaker who lived her whole life in Kansas. There's not one word about how she helped her father build the Panama Canal, or how she lived in a log cabin in Alaska, or went on camera safaris to Africa, or about her grandmother's famous friend, Fanny Crosby. It didn't even mention how she trained her pet pig. Why did you leave out all the good parts?

Your mother's pen pal,

Julie Welsh

May 23

Dear Julie,

Mother's letters to you sprang from her fertile imagination. Had she been born in a different time and place, and married a different man, I believe she would have been a writer of fiction. Instead she led the life that was expected of her, and led it with grace and humor.

When I was young, she told me wonderful stories. Perhaps her letters to you were a way of reliving that happy time in her life.

Please don't be disappointed. She cared a great deal for you.

Best wishes,

Susan Berg

June 12

Dear Susan Berg,

I hope you don't mind another letter from me. I promise I won't bore you with any whining.

At first when I found out that Mrs. Kaplan had made up all those things she wrote to me about, I was angry. I took your letter to school, and my teacher, Mrs. Lumbard, pointed out that our class had learned a lot from Mrs. Kaplan's letters. She reminded me how much fun it had been to look up Fanny Crosby on the Internet, and how we all read books about the Panama Canal and Alaska and Africa. We even learned to appreciate pigs.

Mrs. Lumbard said your mother didn't really lie to me; she just made up stories to enrich my life. I decided that is right.

My class bought a white rosebush and planted it in a redwood planter box. We put it next to Adams Fountain. There is a small brass label on the front of the planter box that's engraved, IN MEMORY OF MRS. KAPLAN. If you are ever near Adams School, I hope you will stop to see the rosebush. It is beautiful.

Ever since we put the rosebush there, the root beer–can maniac has quit leaving empty cans by the fountain. I never found out who it was, and that's okay now that he isn't doing it anymore.

My brother and I competed in the district talent contest. We said the encyclopedia headings as fast as we could. Every time we said one with lots of syllables, such as *Perturbation,* the audience clapped. By the time we finally said *"Zygote!"* the crowd was on its feet.

What a night! We won a big trophy for Adams School. Frankie and I got to present it at a special assembly, and now it's in the trophy case next to Mr. Randolph's office. I look at it every time I go past and I think, Not bad for an average girl.

I have saved my best news for last. My JRA has been better for six weeks! My legs hardly hurt at all and my shoulders and hands are fine, too, even though I quit taking the medication. I had my checkup yesterday, and Dr. McLean says the disease has gone inactive. If a highly respected specialist says my JRA is not active, then it must be true.

I hope I stay this way forever.

Tomorrow is my last day of fifth grade, and my last day at Adams School. I feel happy and sad at the same time.

Your mother's soon-to-be-sixth-grader friend,
Julie Welsh

P.S. Frankie wants to memorize the dictionary this summer. Not me. I'm going to play with Itty Bitty Kitty and roller-skate with my friends.

Author's Note

About 285,000 children in the United States have a form of juvenile arthritis. The most common type is juvenile rheumatoid arthritis (JRA), but there are many other forms. Girls are more likely than boys to have arthritis.

To learn more about juvenile rheumatoid arthritis or related conditions, contact:

American Juvenile Arthritis Foundation
1330 West Peachtree Street
Atlanta, Georgia 30309
(800) 283-7800
http://www.arthritis.org

About the Author

PEG KEHRET's books for young readers are regularly recommended by the American Library Association, the International Reading Association, and the Children's Book Council. She has won "children's choice" book awards in nineteen states and has also won the Golden Kite Award from the Society of Children's Book Writers & Illustrators and the PEN Center West Award for Children's Literature. A longtime volunteer at the Humane Society, she often uses animals in her stories.

Peg and her husband, Carl, live in a log house on ten acres of forest near Mount Rainier National Park. Their property is a sanctuary for blacktail deer, elk, rabbits, and many kinds of birds. They have two grown children, four grandchildren, a dog, and two cats. When she is not writing, Peg likes to read, watch baseball, and pump her old player piano.